To Eve and Evelyn, and the Mojave.

CONTENTS

PREFACE TO THE SECOND EDITION

Thanks to eLectio Publishing for making this second edition of *Edna In The Desert*, the story of a modern teen's first glimpse into adulthood. It explores the widening gap between generations and how our culture is changing with technology. It's a love letter to the Mojave Desert. Also, it's short.

In the second edition, I've had the opportunity to update Apps and technical phrases that I expect will be outdated again soon.

I first thought of Edna after I had interviewed a man for a desert magazine. By choice, he lived remotely, miles from cell phone service, and without a computer. I wondered how a teen might take to this lifestyle as most of my friends' kids are permanently attached to their smart phones. I reflected on how happy I was to have grown up without them, and I thought about a contemporary girl who hadn't.

At thirteen, Edna never had a social life without social media. She played with cell phones before she knew the alphabet. She grew up in a wealthy society that was competitive; a lot was expected of Edna, in school and out. She was smart, and she was a skilled manipulator, or at least she was until recently.

The Mojave Desert is the other inspiration for Edna's story. I wanted to share the inevitable calm and clarity that this breathtaking landscape brings. The setting worked to great advantage in the narrative, which I hope readers continue to enjoy.

—Maddy Lederman
March 2016

EDNA
in the
DESERT

1
THE CURE

The sun baked Edna's forehead and brought her slight queasiness to a more threatening nausea. She tossed over. Changing positions sometimes helped, but pistachios and beef jerky on top of ice cream and the long ride did her in. Or was it what she'd just heard? She didn't remember asking to pull off, only hunching over next to the family's newest, silver Audi. It rocked softly as Brandon bounced around the back. Its motion made her sicker, but Edna tried to stay near the car in its little strip of shade. At eleven in the morning, the sun was already relentless.

"Are you OK, honey?" Edna's mother called from inside.

"What does it look like? Can Brandon stop that?"

The little boy looked out the window at his sister, crouched on the ground and heaving. Edna's father stepped out of the car, saw there was nothing he could do, and stepped back in. The desert was a great place to throw up, and Edna did until there was nothing left. Everything that came out dried almost instantly in the sand. It was so much nicer than putting your head near a toilet, but it didn't seem so nice for the little lizard racing away.

Later, Brandon drooled on his iPad in the back seat. A map rustled up front. The more remote roads were still not on the GPS, and this presented a challenge to Jill, Edna's mother, who had not consulted a paper map in years, not since the last time they came out to her husband's parents' house and got lost. Edward flew out to see them every once in a while, but the tiny airport he landed in was miles in another direction and down completely different dirt roads.

Jill was demoralized by the sight of her thirteen-year-old daughter crumpled in the backseat. Edna was a late bloomer, but she was becoming beautiful. Her wide-set eyes always turned heads, but her personality, left as it was, was going to spoil everything. Jill constantly wondered what she was doing wrong.

"Edna, sit up," prompted no reaction from Edna. "You know, your rebellious stage is a drag."

Jill didn't see when Edna's eyes widened because they were hidden by her palm.

"Can't you see how much trouble you got into this year? Edna, I'm speaking to you."

Edna peeked through her fingers to indicate listening under extreme protest, a gesture Jill ignored.

"Try to sit up. You'll feel better if you sit properly," Jill insisted.

"'Rebellious' implies that I'm rebelling against something when I'm *clearly* ill. You either have a serious lack of sensitivity, or you're sadistic, or just stupid."

Edna was matter-of-fact about it. Jill was speechless. She looked to Edward, who shook his head and offered the usual: "Don't talk to your mother like that," but Edna obviously did.

"Is that all you're going to say?"

Jill knew her husband could assert more authority than that.

"There's no point in arguing anymore. That's why we're doing this."

Edward was one of the rare men who, as far as Edna could see, was the boss of his marriage. As a successful film director, he had a lot of practice manipulating actors, technicians, and studio executives, and Edna's mother didn't stand much of a chance. Jill picked her battles carefully, and this was not going to be one of them. She kept her cool. She had her own life.

Jill was a respected etiquette blogger and highly sought-after public speaker in what Edna considered to be certain uptight circles of privileged ladies whose main concern was how best to please themselves next. Their second concern was purging their collective guilt about the first one by gathering for self-improvement courses, which was where Jill's lifestyle brand, Shimmer, came in. Shimmer dictated the best way to do anything that wasn't a job and purveyed the products needed to do it. Edward wasn't excited about the subject matter, but he was impressed with the amount of money it raked in and all the perks that went along with it.

Because of Shimmer, Jill remained an elegant version of herself at all times. This took work. Her perfect example deterred any of Edna's possible, similar ambition, as opposed to cultivating it, which was the desired effect. Even without any enhancements, Edna thought her mother was gorgeous and intimidating. Lately she'd gotten into the habit of provoking Jill to step outside her notion of appropriate behavior, and if Edna was successful, Jill might raise her voice or let out a scream from inside her shoe closet. Edna wasn't aware that she tortured her mother on purpose; the less perfect Jill became, the closer Edna felt to her. This could be called "negative attention getting," but naming it didn't do any good.

Jill and Edward would tell each other that Edna was "intelligent" and "gifted," but, positive people though they were, these words were hollow. Edna had gone off the charts. Instead of flowering, she'd become combative, impossible to reason with, and there was an embarrassing incident at school involving a pair of dirty gym socks and a teacher's aide. The aide was fired, of course, but when Edward secretly sympathized with the guy, he knew it was time to do *something* about what he laughed off as Edna's severe case of "wiseass-itis."

So, about an hour away from Grandma and Grandpa's, Edna's parents explained: they'd given it a lot of thought and that something would be for Edna to spend the summer in the desert with her grandparents, starting now. Edward told her that her grandmother was a tough woman, and he meant that as a compliment.

Edna's grandparents lived in a small cabin on a large acreage near the town of Desert Palms, California, but Edna wouldn't call it a "town." She'd call it "coordinates on a map." Edna knew that this was at least partially because of the sock incident and that, in fact, her father blamed her for it. It was so unfair. If someone doesn't know the difference between "strained" and "sprained," they should not have

3

authority in a school. Besides, the act was clearly premeditated; no one could fish socks out of their gym bag that quickly. Edna would have the memory of that lunatic charging at her and the smell and taste of his filthy socks burned into her brain for life, but that didn't seem to matter to anyone.

Edna whimpered things like "the whole summer?" and "it's not my fault!" and that she "would be really good," but she was still too sarcastic, and it didn't matter what she said anymore anyway. Her parents had undertaken a military-like approach to this maneuver, and they were not turning back.

"I want you to be an exceptional woman, Edna, and I want you to be yourself," Jill explained, "but you're always out to prove something. You'll find that not everyone appreciates your constant one-upmanship, certainly not Grandma."

"What's the problem, exactly? 'One-upmanship' or that your words are poorly chosen and you don't know what rebellious means, and I simply take the trouble to point it out?"

"The problem is that you're a...word that rhymes with witch—"

"Edward!"

"She needs to know how she's perceived."

Jill couldn't deny that she'd called Edna the same thing, but not directly to her. She didn't immediately agree to leave Edna in the desert when Edward presented the idea. He refused to put Edna on medication, and there was increasing pressure from the therapist to send her to a psychiatrist. It was time to do something radical, he explained. After Edna handed a bottle of mouthwash to the genius she'd worked so hard to get for piano lessons, Jill agreed. The award-winning pianist was insulted and embarrassed, and he never came back.

"Edna, you have no respect for others. It can't go on, and it's not going to be tolerated," Jill said.

"If it can't go on, it won't need to be tolerated. You're getting illogical—"

"And you're getting a lot of time to think."

Her father's tone was sharp enough to end the exchange.

Edna pictured herself trapped in her grandparents' dreary world. She was no longer sure if she was breathing. Hopefully she would pass out quickly and die. Until then she couldn't reveal any further weakness. Perhaps if she seemed happy about this idea it wouldn't seem like enough of a punishment, and her parents might change their minds. She could only hope that there was no way they were serious and that this was merely a sadistic joke, but the main challenge at the moment was to keep from crying.

Garbled in the background, while this momentous challenge was underway, was Jill's voice suggesting that Edna do her best to get on well with Grandma.

"—and try not to worry about Grandpa. He can hear, I think, and he can stand up. The way to be a good guest, Edna, is to be cheerful, to offer help, and to never need to be entertained."

Edna had no idea why Grandpa liked to sit on the porch for the entire day, but that was his story, and she certainly didn't expect Grandpa to entertain her. Sometimes it looked like he was going to get up, but usually that was a cough or a sneeze, and it almost always disgusted Edna. He ate on a TV tray that Grandma brought, and at the end of the day he'd come inside and go to bed. It never occurred to Edna that that had been going on, all this time, since she was last there two years ago. Edna didn't like to think about Grandpa, and she hardly ever did.

"Grandma and Grandpa came to live out here because Grandpa was very sick. That was a...a long time ago, before you were born, but many years after Grandpa fought in a war that—"

Edward told Jill not to make it so complicated.

This was the speech Jill had been selling to make Grandma and Grandpa seem more human. It was all starting to make sense: the speeches, the snacks, the ice cream in the morning. This kidnapping scheme disguised as a fun little trip was not appreciated. Edna might have at least packed her clothes or said good-bye to her friends. Instead she was going to disappear like some freak.

"Grandma and Grandpa have a phone now," Jill reminded her.

It was a landline. Edna's grandparents had just acquired a 100-year-old technology. It was not likely that they also had Internet. Or a computer. Edna checked her phone, a useless, pink object with games on it and no service. For all practical purposes, Edna had died. She didn't know if she'd ever fully recover from this; she'd just gotten things perfect after changing schools over some other problem that was totally not her fault either.

"Edna, you have to be a little brave. It's a hard life. Grandma has no place to go. There's no one around, there's nowhere to go to dinner—"

Edward interrupted to point out that there were a couple of restaurants, not that Grandma and Grandpa go out very much, and a few stores.

Edna silently gasped against her carsickness and the future. She rested her head by the window so air could rush over her face. The rhythmic whir of the wheels on the road gave her something else to focus on. Creosote bushes whipped past, creating streaks of green ribbon in the sand, and the road sloped up into forever, the low horizon line ahead promising an ocean of anything beyond it. Even though hell and, hopefully, a swift and merciful death were in that direction, it was beautiful and Edna was hypnotized. For a moment the whole family was.

2
DESERTED

The Audi floated up the dirt road that led to Grandma and Grandpa's cabin, which was, for some reason, built in the middle of nowhere. There wasn't another house or building in sight. Edna was about to spend a lot of time contemplating why Grandma and Grandpa lived where they did and wishing they lived somewhere exciting like San Francisco or New York City or London. She wondered whether, if they lived somewhere fun, this punishment would have been the same. Probably not. She wondered what worse things her parents could've come up with, but nothing she thought of distracted her enough. Panic still firmly gripped her chest.

A coyote crossed the road ahead as if they didn't exist. This was clearly his desert and nobody else's. Edna resented him for making the car slow down, prolonging the suspense for another second or two, when the dreaded shack appeared in the distance. Flanked by two stately eucalyptus trees, a dilapidated garage, and some kind of tank on stilts, the ramshackle structure was little more than a wooden tent. As they moved closer, a speck on the porch became the silhouette of Grandpa, immobile in his chair. The entire scenario was exactly the same as it had been two years ago, except two years ago Edna knew she'd be leaving in an hour. The strong figure of Grandma emerged from inside. Her hands fell to her hips like a five-star general, and her creased, emotionless face emerged in the sun.

Edna was not ashamed to admit that she preferred her other grandmother. Nanny did yoga, played bridge and ran her tennis league. None of that would be going on here. Here, there was only the blaring sky and the hard gaze of an unfriendly old woman.

The car came to a stop. Edna considered her options. She could refuse to move, but the image of her limbs flailing around while her father pulled her from the car was distasteful. She knew he could physically overpower her. She could jump into the driver's seat in an attempt to speed off, but even if she had the key to the car, she'd be caught frantically pressing buttons, trying to remember how to drive before she could get away. And how far could she go? She'd never driven outside of an empty parking lot. Her failed escape attempt would not set things off on the right foot with Grandma if the unthinkable happened and she was left here. Edna wished her heart would explode like it felt it was going to, or that she could think of something to do. For the moment, she had to march through this charade until she cornered one of her parents separately in an attempt to break their resolve. Her father was already taking her suitcase out of the trunk, and her mother greeted Grandma.

"I always forget how beautiful the drive here is," Jill gushed. "We saw a coyote run right by us on the way in. Do they bother you much?"

"Not much," Grandma replied and then said, "He got big," referring to Brandon. "Come in, I got some drinks for you."

She walked into the house. She had not so much as glanced in Edna's direction. Jill stiffened a little and, with Edward and Brandon, she followed Grandma inside. Edna lingered on the porch in the eerie quiet, hoping one of her parents would come scold her for being antisocial. Then she could start chipping away at the situation. Neither of them did. She searched the open desert for what Grandpa seemed so interested in.

"Hi Grandpa," she offered with a nervous lilt.

Grandpa's silence was creepy enough to make Edna feel like going inside.

The "big room" was both a living room and a kitchen. It had a wood stove. A door off this room went to her grandparents' bedroom. It was open a crack and dark inside, which was weird in the brightness of the day. A room on the other side of the big room was where Edna would sleep. She didn't think it was possible, but her heart sank even further. Edna didn't remember this room because it was actually a large pantry. It was old and dusty and not good enough for one night, much less a whole summer. Jill came in, and Edna's horror was conveniently underscored by Brandon, who blurted out:

"Wow, what a crap room!"

Grandma and Grandpa's pantry was crammed with shelves and stocked with enough cans and bulk items for the end of the world they may have been planning for. An army cot was shoved into a corner.

"I'd rather be in jail. At least a prison cell wouldn't be cluttered," Edna said, in spite of the lump in her throat, and she folded her arms. Brandon squealed and jumped on the cot.

"Brandon, go to the car and get your sister's blanket," Jill demanded. "Speed demon!" The little boy darted off as the speed of light with sound effects.

"Edna, do you think this is easy for Grandma?"

"No. I think it's a terrible imposition, and one we shouldn't be making."

Brandon rushed back with Edna's pink and orange blanket, and, ever the "speed demon," he zipped away. Edna was sure that her colorful blanket, while not quite alive, would die in this drab environment. Edward brought in more of Edna's clothes and some books that were secretly packed in the trunk, the whole conspiracy now revealed. He looked for a place to set things down, and not finding a good one, he put them on some empty metal drums that were rusty and would surely ruin Edna's clothes. Jill emptied out the drawers of a sideboard and put Edna's clothes away while Edward tried to organize the toxic pesticides, among other ancient household items, that came out of the drawers. Edna felt the environment spoke for itself, and she didn't lift a finger to help them settle her into it.

Moments later they all sat around the table for what Grandma called a glass of "pop." Jill chatted away as if she had the power to smooth over this unseemly situation. Grandma showed the little interest she'd mustered as best she could. Seeing these two women, it became clear to Edna that her father loved her mother as a reaction to his own mother's dour disposition. They were all acting normally, as if there wasn't some kind of sick child-abuse scam in effect. Edna couldn't process much that was said while still trying to conjure a way out of this. She caught part of a conversation: Brandon asked Grandma where her TV was, and Jill explained that Grandma didn't have a TV. That being too horrible to imagine, the boy let it drop and answered boring questions about kindergarten that Jill asked him for the benefit of informing Grandma.

Edna invited her father to speak with her outside so she could persuade him that depriving her of horseback-riding camp and the use of her phone (except for two hours a day) would be equally as punitive as the current plan.

"Be right out," he said, and he disappeared into the bathroom.

Edna had no opportunity to present her alternative; her parents jumped into the car as if they'd just robbed a bank. They'd clearly planned to drop her and take off, avoiding an unpleasant drama. The Audi's wheels spun out as it got up to speed. Jill looked back from inside. Edna felt some satisfaction seeing her mother's doubt about this bizarre plot already setting in. The car drifted away across the sand, and only a cloud of dust lingered after it jumped over the horizon. They were gone.

One final possibility occurred to Edna before she would succumb to the idea that she'd been left behind: this could be a very well-executed trick, the sadistic joke she'd imagined it must be earlier. Her parents were more than capable of such a simple prank. The threat of this punishment was a punishment in itself; there was *no way* they could possibly do it. A trick made much more sense, and a wave of relief washed over Edna. It was funny how serious her mother looked; she even overacted a bit. Edna was convinced that the Audi would come back over the horizon to whisk her away in a minute or two.

She'd tell her parents how sorry she was about everything. She'd be more careful about provoking people like the teacher's aide, even though he was probably mentally disabled and therefore lacked an adult level of restraint. While thinking of the most diplomatic way of putting this, Edna got lost in a conversation with herself: If she could learn the difference between "strained" and "sprained," why couldn't he? She hadn't done anything wrong in expecting he'd know the difference between muscles and ligaments, especially if he was teaching gym. To tell the truth, Edna had no idea what she might be sorry for, other than pointing this out a few too many times. Or ten too many times. But he shouldn't have lost control, and there were witnesses. The school wouldn't have fired him if there were any doubt about his guilt.

Maybe her parents were still mad about the Mondell incident. Edna thought they'd all moved on. Ms. Mondell taught physical science, but that was no excuse for her disastrous grammar. Edna might have been wrong for correcting her every mistake, but it had nothing to do with the volcano experiment. She was sent to the principal anyway, and it was decided it would be best if she changed classes. If someone else had caused an explosion, Edna was sure Ms. Mondell would have understood it was an accident. Otherwise, there was only Mrs. Carson in Girl Scouts and that disgusting piano teacher.

Soon Edna noticed that the Audi had not returned. She saw little point in refining her defense. She waited longer than she thought her father would before turning back, which got to be longer and longer as she desperately recalculated how far he might go to trick her. She tried to ignore her heart's wild pounding. A flat hum set in, and then a profound bleakness seeped into Edna's spirit. No one was coming back for her anytime soon. She was suffocating even though she could breathe. She was not alone, with Grandpa on the porch, but he made her feel like there was less than nobody there. A few specks on the distant hills looked like houses, but after lingering on them, Edna could see they were big rocks. The space was infinite, but it was just as confining as the tiniest jail cell.

3
EDNA VS. GRANDMA

Edna took stock of her surroundings: Grandpa in his wooden chair, two eucalyptus trees in front of the porch, and wind. Nothing else. She'd been at this crossroads once already, namely, whether to stand out here with Grandpa or go inside. It was about to become one of her few considerations for the foreseeable future. Edna had never felt this desperate before. She was surprised that this desperate feeling did not cause the world to end. Things were still going on. Things still needed to be done.

She had to go in and acknowledge Grandma. Waiting any longer would be uncivilized and only make things worse. She might try to act like this was going to be a fun visit, but, ambushed and defeated, Edna knew she couldn't pull it off. With no time to think, she walked into the house without a plan and feeling vulnerable.

Edna had a second to observe Grandma while she washed glasses and was turned away from the door. Her long, gray hair was shiny and held back in a ponytail. The energy she put into her body made her look bigger. She said, "I heard there's been some trouble at school," without turning around, and then:

"Come dry these and put them away."

Her skin was leathery from the desert. Edna approached her with an almost insulting amount of caution. Grandma handed her a dish towel and then went to the bedroom. Edna dried the glasses, and her face heated up as the new reality of being left in this dismal cabin set in. She had no idea where to put the glasses when they were dry. There were only four cabinets. Their old, wooden doors were worn out around the knobs. She opened one of them. Grandma reappeared with laundry, said, "No, top right" and went outside.

Edna knew her grandmother wasn't an affectionate person, but she was surprised that she'd not planned anything to welcome her, even if this "visit" was supposed to be some kind of punishment.

Maybe Grandma was insulted that being at her house was considered a punishment. It wasn't exactly a compliment.

Edna took in her grandparents' home. The living area was furnished with a coffee table that was finished to look like wood and two sections of a shapeless, fake leather couch in the grayest shade of pink possible. On it were crochet pillows made with yarn in a rainbow of colors. Edna found them dreadful. A plastic palm tree sat on the coffee table and another one was on a windowsill. This could be the waiting room of a free clinic in a bad neighborhood. It made no sense: Why did her grandparents live in this depressing place? And how could she stay here? She'd never make it through an hour, never mind a whole summer. Edna lost the fight to hold back her tears; this was going to be a bad cry. She rushed into the pantry, tripped over a wooden crate and scratched her leg on a rusty nail. It bled. She didn't care. She fell onto her army cot and into a cry that went on so long her stomach hurt, and then it went on longer.

As much as the situation warranted extended crying, eventually Edna couldn't anymore. She couldn't think anymore either. It was so quiet, she couldn't hear a sound. She wondered what Grandma was doing. After a while she was distracted by the objects in the pantry. She found an old bottle of witch hazel and put some on her cut. She studied Grandma's shelves. Canned hash, canned ham, and Spam were at first gross and then horrific when Edna realized this would probably be her food. She hadn't even thought of food. She wondered if Jill told Grandma what she liked to eat, but she doubted Grandma would care if she had.

Edna decided that there was no way she could eat Spam, and if she had to she didn't want to live anymore. She'd said "I'm going to kill myself" throughout her life, more times than she could remember, but she'd never really meant it or thought about how. She knew she couldn't kill herself violently—she was too afraid of pain—but she might be serious about wanting to for the first time. She checked the medicine cabinet in the bathroom. It had no pills that would be lethal, only aspirin. Nanny was on tons of medication, and so was everyone at her condo. Edna was surprised her grandparents had none. She couldn't have taken their pills anyway. It was too scary. If you didn't die, you could end up permanently sick.

Her grandparents' bathroom was tiled in a soft, sky blue. At eye level, one row was decorated with surfers riding a wave. The cheery, nautical scene had nothing in common with its bleak surroundings. Edna listened to the wind rattle the windowpanes.

She went back to her cot in the cluttered pantry. She was wishing she could just disappear and not have to exist for the summer when she remembered something from a documentary, one her mother forced her to watch so she'd be more worldly. Worldliness was important to Jill, which was ironic to Edna, since she thought her mother was extremely insulated and provincial. In an obscure Tibetan documentary, a room full of monks made themselves sweat while they sat still for hours. Eventually steam came off their bodies, even in cold temperatures. This inspired Shimmer's version of meditation, as that was becoming a huge trend. Jill called it a "spiritual detox" and held classes in a hot yoga studio. She already had a six-month waiting list.

In any case, Edna wondered if she could sweat enough to make herself completely evaporate. It was an edgy, forward-thinking idea. Human beings were, after all, mostly made of water. She knew thoughts could change the molecules of water as she'd seen this in a different documentary. Edna thought evaporating herself could be a painless process. No one would ever know what had become of her. It might be the perfect escape. It was certainly hot enough to try it, and she had absolutely nothing else to do.

She sat very still on the cot and called upon all her cells to disconnect from each other, to float away, making her body a fine vapor rising upward. It was the best way she could picture it, and visualizing things helped in sports and gymnastics. She wondered if the desert being so dry might make evaporating any easier. Focusing as hard as she could for what must have been at least five minutes did not result in any part of her body evaporating, not even a little skin. She tried it for a little longer.

It occurred to Edna that a hunger strike would be easier than mastering the complex energy that held her molecules together and would also eliminate the possible ingestion of canned meats. A hunger strike had the added benefit of letting her live beyond the summer, if she could live without food for two months, and it would make a strong statement about this terrible injustice. Political prisoners went on hunger strikes. A hunger strike sounded much better than evaporating, and she could start one at any time. Maybe she'd already started it.

Edna thought her parents really overdid it by leaving her with books about pioneer women of the Old West and nothing else. They must have been planning this for weeks. It probably brought them together; it was disgusting. Their backstabbing trick would certainly damage Edna's trust in them forever. She might let them think there was a chance she'd ever trust them again, but only so they'd keep trying to make it up to her with gifts. In the meantime, killing herself might be unnecessary if she could at least read. She'd get to live the rest of her life and have gifts to look forward to. Maybe things weren't going to be so bad. Edna was impressed with her ability to conjure a positive attitude when Grandma came in and ruined it.

"I don't know what your parents told you—"

"They didn't tell me anything. Staying here was a complete surprise that I found out about five minutes before we arrived. I'm sure I was the last person to know about it. My parents are lucky I don't report them to the police for abduction or kidnapping. In fact, I think I might."

Grandma noted Edna's personality problem as it had been described to her weeks earlier.

"You're going to shape up this summer, Edna, and that will not include reading all day."

"What else is there to do around here?"

Edna didn't even close her book. Grandma was not impressed.

"The best thing you can do for yourself, Edna, is to follow me."

Grandma left. Edna was in fighting mode, but there was no point in starting things off quite so badly. Still, she moved off the cot as slowly as she could with the intention of exerting some pittance of power over Grandma by making her wait a few extra seconds. Grandma didn't seem to notice. She was seated in the big room and finishing a list when Edna came in.

"Grandpa and I don't like too much company. I don't think we ever had any, except your dad and you all, and some doctors."

This sounded really depressing. If things were about to get worse, Edna knew anything she might say would probably make it worse than that. She was in foreign territory. The new strategy was to keep quiet and observe. She could have saved herself a lot of trouble by discovering this strategy sooner, and the realization came with some regret. Instead of being here, she should be at the Grove sipping bubble tea and getting friendship bracelets. Everyone was at the mall after school was over and before they left for camp.

"We love you as our grandchild, Edna, but that isn't going to make it fun around here, in case you were expecting that," Grandma informed her.

Edna wasn't.

"I'm making a list of things to do, regular chores and a few side projects. I don't care which one you start with, but you will spend your time productively, not lying around entertaining yourself all day."

Edna decided against debating the nuanced meanings of productivity with Grandma. She would have jumped all over the topic with her parents.

"It's fine to read and watch television and be a smarty-pants, but you have to back it up with something."

Edna had no idea how watching television had anything to do with being smart. The summer continued its downward spiral, with slave labor added to captivity, isolation and canned meat. Maybe she could just walk out into the desert, die of thirst and skip the boring evaporation attempts or lengthy hunger strikes. She could run away at any time, but Edna wasn't sure she had the courage to do it. Maybe she could try to do the list. Grandma didn't wait to see Edna's reaction to it; she went back to her laundry.

Grandma's handwriting was small and hard to read. Edna was sure this was intentional. The paper said: *House rules: I do the cooking. Don't bother Grandpa. Things to do: Washing and drying dishes and putting them away. Sweeping. Dusting. Mopping floor. Taking rugs out and beating them, every week. Keeping weeds away from the swamp cooler and the house. Bathroom—clean all. Clean out the garage. Paint the porch. Make a cement patio…maybe too hard. Laundry two or three times a week. Wash out cans for recycling.*

Did her parents have any idea of this program? Judging by the amount of books they brought, Edna guessed not. They needed to be told. Edna found Grandma's phone in the kitchen area. It looked like it should be on an old movie set, like everything else in the cabin.

Before Edna called them, she built her argument: forcing her to do these chores and hard labor out in the desert heat was a physical threat. What was the difference between this level of discomfort and a violent beating that her parents could be arrested for? And how could she emotionally evolve under such conditions, with her survival constantly at risk? If she was to really improve, she needed time for spiritual reflection, and she needed to reflect in a safe environment, not in a scary place with these creepy, old strangers. Edna would propose she be grounded for the entire summer and have a strict spiritual retreat at home instead. She could even pitch the idea as a "pray-cation," and Jill could blog about it on Shimmer. Edna would make her mother think she thought of it herself. They could post pictures: Edna in robes like a monk, serenely reflected in their pool, in front of the waterfall they put in last year. Jill could promote her contractor in the photo's caption. She loved to promote people and get them work. Edna suspected this was an attempt to collect favors and brandish power. Regardless, Edna was sure she could convince her mother that a "pray-cation" was the perfect solution and long overdue.

She had to make her call in the big room from the phone attached to the wall, and she didn't care what Grandma thought if she overheard anything. In fact, she wanted Grandma to know exactly who she was dealing with. She picked up the phone and heard what she remembered was called a "dial tone." That meant the phone worked. Good. It had a rotary dial, something Edna had never used before, but she'd seen it done. She had both her parents' numbers memorized. She dialed her father. She always confronted him before her mother because if he said "yes," it meant "yes" and not "maybe," and then she didn't have to ask twice. The call went to voice mail. Her mother's phone also went to voice mail. Despicable. They'd easily driven far enough to have service. Edna was sure it must be a crime to drop your daughter in the middle of nowhere and then not answer your phone.

When she put the receiver in its cradle, she noticed an army of ants crawling up the wall. They made a perfect line. As neat as they were, they still made Edna's skin crawl. There were probably ants and bugs all over this place, and especially in that pantry she was supposed to be sleeping in. Edna had no idea what to do about the ants, or her parents. In the meantime, these chores were so out of bounds, Edna wasn't sure if she even had to listen to Grandma. What would happen if she tore up the list and read a book all day? What could Grandma really do about it?

Edna had a habit of making broad, dramatic gestures, which was one of the reasons why she was often in trouble and left in the desert. She thoroughly tore up Grandma's list. It felt good to rail against these incredible circumstances, and she ripped the paper into the tiniest pieces she could. She heard Grandma's footsteps on the porch.

Edna hadn't thought about Grandma seeing this, but it was too late to hide the scraps of paper all around her. Grandma looked shocked, and Edna was glad, but Grandma was only temporarily thrown. She took out a key, went to the pantry door and locked it. She put the key back in her pocket. Then she went into the bathroom, came out with some towels and walked out.

Edna dashed to the door and tried not to rattle it too loudly while she desperately yanked on the doorknob. Now Edna knew what Grandma could do if she tore up that list: she could lock her out of the pantry and leave her with nothing but the clothes she had on, with nothing to do in a boring room.

Edna sat on the ugly couch, stunned. She had to admit that Grandma's tactic was a surprise and rather cunning. With no access to her things, Edna could sit and stare the day away or do the dreadful list of chores. Only Grandma hadn't counted on Edna's third option.

4
DYING IN THE DESERT

Edna had seen people die in the desert in movies, so she had some idea of what to expect. They just walked until they passed out. It wouldn't be hard to kill herself this way, she imagined, because she didn't have to do anything. It would just happen. She cut a beeline into the harsh landscape ahead. She was in full view of Grandpa, but he wasn't likely to stop her. The scrub brush scratched at her ankles, and the sun brought back her headache from earlier in the car. It was hard to believe, with all that had happened, that this was still the same day.

Escape was empowering and, like a determined warrior, Edna pressed further and further, each step a manifestation of her spirited defiance. Grandma and Grandpa's property became small behind her, and the tall eucalyptus trees disappeared as she dropped into the valley.

Edna saw her own funeral: her mother in black, grief-stricken and barely able to stand by the grave. She leaned on Edward, who stood strong, but tears cracked his fortress of stoicism and etched paths down his face. Both her parents knew that they'd killed their own child with neglect, and in fact, charges were pending. Brandon cried and asked when he could see his big sister again, sharpening everyone's profound sadness. The scene itself wept, dripping with stunning, white flowers in passionate arrangements.

A flock of sniffling young teens in black would gather around Edna's newest best friend, Brit, and only say good things about Edna. Saying anything negative about a dead person would be viewed as extremely uncool, especially at their funeral. It's amazing what it takes to stop people from talking behind other people's backs, Edna noted. She imagined what nice things her friends might say about her because they had to say something. She knew she was smart, and she tried hard to be good at things. She was funny sometimes. There must be something better to say than that. It disturbed her that she didn't know what it was. She expected her school to start a scholarship in her honor because they always did that when someone died. The stupid teacher's aide would come forward and admit that he'd attacked Edna, not because she did anything wrong but because he'd forgotten to take his medication, making her death caused by a too-severe punishment for the incident all the more poignant.

A priest would make his eulogy, highlighting how terribly Edna had been treated by her parents, starting with the fact that they had named her "Edna" (her father's name was "Edward," but that wasn't a good enough reason; they could have named Brandon "Edward") and leading all the way to today. Finally, the police would come and arrest her parents in front of everyone. They'd be escorted from their daughter's funeral in handcuffs. That night they'd find themselves in jail, and only then would they have an inkling of what it felt like for Edna to be left out here in the middle of nowhere, in barely a house, with two extremely weird old people.

After wandering for so long, Edna was thirsty. A child of overachieving parents, she'd been very well-hydrated all her life, so she believed the thirsty feeling must mean she'd be dying fairly soon. At this point Edna thought she should find a place to lie down, but the ground was covered with prickly brush that seemed like it might hurt. And it was too hot to lie in the sun. Edna might be dying, but there was no point in being uncomfortable.

She'd pictured someplace more romantic, perhaps with trees on a small hill, in which to die. Of course in the desert, it would be too much to expect a pretty little pond to lie next to. And then it would be silly to die of thirst next to a pond. Nothing was making sense. In spite of what she could see in all directions, Edna hoped she might at least stumble upon some kind of rock formation that might provide shade and look good in pictures on the news. Edna walked and walked. She eventually came to the conclusion that she was not going to find the perfect place to die, or even a good one.

If it wasn't going to be artful, Edna was no longer sure she was interested in dying. Also, was this hideous salmon dress her mother forced her into this morning really what she wanted to be found dead in? With her hair up in a ponytail? Worse, she had nothing to write with, so there would be no note. She hadn't considered the importance of a note when she stormed away from the cabin. There had to be a note. Without it, it could look like she had taken a walk and died by accident. Without a note her political agenda was gone. She might be remembered as an idiot who got lost. The more she looked around, the more she realized the desert was a sea of sameness, and even with a note it was unlikely that anyone might find her, a pale, salmon needle in an endless, sandy haystack. Edna had no idea where she was. Neither did anyone else.

She hadn't seen the eucalyptus trees for some time. Now she was really thirsty. She didn't have a hat, and she had not recently applied sunscreen. She'd had enough of this walk, as it was now redefined, but at the moment she was definitely lost. And definitely scared. An ominous wind whistled, and the horizon seemed further away. She had never been so completely alone before in her life. Edna didn't have the slightest idea what to do next, and nothing in the unfamiliar world hinted at an answer.

The stillness lasted far too long, until a snake hissed and sent Edna into the air with a scream. Her scream floated across the basin. It attracted no one's attention. Screams were not unlike thirst in Edna's life, in that they always commanded some nearby adult's immediate attention. Nothing stood between her and this dangerous creature, but her scream must have scared it because it slithered away. She moved swiftly in the opposite direction, scrub brush attacking her ankles with every step. The snake was gone, but he was fast; he could easily change his mind and come back. What if there were other snakes all around her?

The faraway hills looked the same in every direction. The sun wasn't exactly in the middle of the sky, but she had no idea what that meant in terms of Grandma and Grandpa's cabin. She had been so busy thinking about her funeral the entire time she had been walking, she didn't notice if the sun was on her face or behind her. She settled under a creosote bush; dappled sun was the closest thing to shade. The world fell into that stillness. She felt dangerously exposed, yet trapped. Her breath became shallow and quick, and her lungs tightened as she fought to open them with air. She wondered if a person could suddenly get asthma from being afraid. Prickly cactus needles stabbed her butt cheek. Frustrated, Edna sprang up and brushed them off.

She tried to recognize the purple hills or something that would indicate she should go a certain way. Nothing did. She paced back and forth to see if the eucalyptus trees might appear. She thought it was better to stay put if you were lost, but she wasn't even sure if she remembered that right. Edna had experienced fear in her life, but not like this. Crying only wasted water, she thought, as she caught her breath between sobs. It didn't make her know what to do or how to change anything in the desert.

5
STILL DYING

Edna woke up with one side of her face in the sand and the other side sunburned. She wasn't sure how long she'd slept. In front of her, the roundest, cutest little bunny was huddled under another creosote bush. He had a perfect cotton-ball tail. The bunny was looking at her sideways with just one of his eyes. Edna liked his company. Somehow the bunny was company. She allowed herself to take in the full cuteness of him. His brown hairs were short and shiny. He was still a baby and breathing quickly, like a small bird. Like she was breathing. She could see the shape of his tiny elbow bone poking into his fur. She wished she could pet him, but she didn't think he'd stay if she put her hand out. They looked at each other for a long time. It was so quiet, Edna could hear the blood pulsing through her ears. The wind and the empty hum of the desert world had gone away. Then the bunny scampered off for a reason Edna would never know.

Now Edna was lonely in addition to dirty, hungry, thirsty, and sunburned. She'd never had a sunburn before, but she knew she had one now because her cheek stung.

Thirst was a priority. She wondered where in the world that bunny got water around here. The only things that seemed to have any moisture were the tiny creosote leaves. She picked some off and chewed them. They were sticky with a bitter, terrible taste, and they didn't seem to be delivering any amount of water. Edna spit them out but her mouth was dry, and the green gunk landed on her chin. Wiping it off, she figured she'd lost water trying that, and they might have been poison, too. It would be too ironic if she died, after she'd decided not to. Edna really didn't want to die, and she was surprised she ever thought she did. She had to admit that she'd just hoped to upset her parents and her grandmother in the worst way possible. Her death would certainly hurt them, but she hadn't considered the personal cost and the discomfort of dying. She would think of better ways to upset these people in the future, ones that wouldn't be so treacherous and inconvenient. Now she needed to focus on this

25

problem of being lost. She tried to think of it as a problem that could be solved, though she didn't know if it was, because once she succumbed to her mounting fear she'd be in bigger trouble. Edna might die of a heart attack from that as much as anything else.

The sun hovered over the hills. While she no longer wanted to die, she was as close as she'd ever been to doing so. There might be more snakes when it got dark, or scorpions. If she hadn't been kicked out of Girl Scouts for being "provocative and disrespectful," Edna might have had some idea. Her mind was dimming too much to relive that injustice. She didn't notice the brush scraping against her ankles anymore. She needed to stay alert if she was to have a chance of surviving a night in the wilderness, but instead she was faint and disoriented. A low, buzzing sound emerged, and she thought it must have been coming from inside her head. Then it sounded like the wind, but Edna saw no wind; all the creosote bushes were still. Soon it sounded like the ocean, but that was impossible. She had become convinced that her brain was falling apart when what was making the sound became clear to her.

She was standing next to a swarm of flies buzzing around a decomposing coyote carcass. If Edna had known what she was going to see, she never would have looked in that direction. The coyote's ribcage was exposed, like a fan sticking up out of its pink, bloody flesh. The poor thing's head rested at a weird angle to the side. Adrenaline shot through her torso as Edna dashed away from the gruesome sight. A hawk or a vulture, she didn't know what it was, circled lazily overhead. This was all a little too real. Edna might try to stage her own lovely death, but here was a firsthand account of what it basically came down to.

Edna was stumbling, sobbing, and certain she was hallucinating when another buzzing sound got louder. It was different from the last one; it sounded more like a lawnmower. Who could be mowing a lawn out here? Her eyes darted around the landscape, but it was empty as ever. Louder still, the sound was coming from behind her. Edna spun around and saw a stream of dust rising across the basin. The moving dust veered toward her.

6
THE BOY

The dirt bike zipped through the basin toward Edna. The boy wore a titanium helmet, a white T-shirt and jeans. What was he doing out here? Edna had no idea if he was nice or would help her. He was more likely a meth freak or some kind of criminal. There would be nothing to stop him from hurting her if he wanted to, least of all the depleted and defenseless Edna. He stopped the bike a few yards away from her and took off his helmet.

"Hey."

He kneeled down to a compartment on the bike. He was unaware of his appearance or its effect on her. Before Edna was the best-looking boy she'd ever seen, and Edna grew up in Hollywood. She'd seen a lot of handsome boys. He had dark hair, steel-blue eyes and high cheekbones. He was thin and tan and dusted from riding the bike.

"Here."

He handed her a bottle of water. The world was a very different place than it had been thirty seconds ago. A young god had appeared, with water. Edna was mystified.

"You're Edna, right?"

Her eyes were swollen from crying, one half of her face was burned and the other was speckled with the sand she'd slept in. She nodded.

"Yes."

The word cracked as it came out of her throat. She didn't know it was so dry she could barely speak. The water was astonishing, cool and delicious. She tried not to gulp it too hard, but some spilled out of the corners of her mouth.

"Are you OK?"

Edna coughed.

"I think so."

"You can't just wander out into the desert by yourself, you know. It's not safe."

"I know that."

There was no point in defending her position. She'd fully intended to put herself in danger in the first place.

"I got lost."

"Well, you're found now."

His voice was deep, and he had the slightest rural twang.

"Here."

He gave her a hand wipe for her face. Edna was sunburned and thirsty but otherwise fine. All the fear she'd kept bottled up escaped, and she let a few tears fall.

"I saw a dead coyote," she explained.

"There's a lot of dead stuff out here."

He turned and spoke into a radio on the bike.

"This is Johnny. I found her, Wayne."

An older man's voice came through.

"Great news!"

A smattering of cheers rang out. Edna began to understand that Johnny was part of a search for her, that emergency services had been called and also probably her parents.

"Where are you?" Wayne asked.

"Way northwest in the basin."

"OK, well—"

Someone yelled out something in the background.

"Shut up! OK, just come back in, Johnny."

He handed Edna a helmet.

"Let's get you back. Oh, I'm Johnny. You probably guessed."

Edna was totally in awe of him and too weak to hide it. He would definitely think she was weird, if he didn't already. After all, she'd wandered into the desert and almost killed herself. Anyway, why did she care what he thought? She was rescued. She tried to focus on adjusting the helmet's straps, but she was oddly uncoordinated and incapable of doing it.

"I'm Edna, but you already knew that," she blurted out, then managed to look up. "Thank you for saving me."

"No problem."

His smile both relaxed and excited her. It gave her a little shot of adrenaline, but it was sweet, not scary like the one she got from seeing the coyote. All of a sudden, what someone else thought of her really mattered to Edna. She was frozen with no idea how to act, afraid this boy might not like her the way she was, since everyone, including her own parents, called her a brat.

Finally helmeted, she got onto the back of Johnny's bike. There was nothing to hold onto except him. She put her arms around his waist with just enough time to stay put before he sped off. The ride was uncomfortable and bumpy, the motor was loud and normally Edna wouldn't have thought this was fun at all. From what she knew of dirt biking, it was a meaningless, environmentally unsound sport that wasted gas.

Johnny moved a lot as he weaved around the cactus and the brush. He was good at it. She tried not to hold onto him too tightly, but it was a fine line between that and staying on the bike. Going over a bigger bump, she felt his muscles flex as he steadied it. She became lightheaded. It could have been hunger. She hadn't eaten a thing since she threw up the pistachio nuts.

Soon Grandma and Grandpa's cabin glowed in the dusk ahead. A battle unfolded in the sky as the blue night rose up behind the hills and devoured the glowing band of pink above it. With the vision, the bike's noise and Johnny's torso, euphoria radiated through Edna. She'd never felt this alive before. She'd never get lost in the desert again, but this one time it was worth it.

Cars were parked around her grandparents' cabin, and boys and men loaded dirt bikes onto a flatbed. As they got closer, Edna noticed a sheriff's car.

"Is that the police?"

"Your grandmother had to call someone. She couldn't exactly find you by herself."

Johnny sped up in a clearing. What Grandma would do when she found Edna missing hadn't occurred to her because it wasn't supposed to matter. She'd jumped way ahead to her funeral.

As they pulled up to the cabin, a flash went off.

"Hi, Tom," Johnny said.

"Great get," the man taking pictures answered.

They coasted past Grandpa, still in his chair on the dimly lit porch. Edna didn't like that everyone could see there was something wrong with her grandfather, but it was a lesser concern of the moment; she had Grandma to think about. She didn't have the energy left to be as afraid of her as she might have been earlier. Johnny remarked that it looked like Edna had made the newspaper on her first day in the desert, and Grandma replied that it didn't take much to get into *The Desert Weekly*. She didn't look at Edna. Edna found this unnerving. An older man in a sheriff's uniform approached.

"So you're our Edna?"

"Yes. Thank you for finding me," Edna answered in a voice that sounded so sweet she wasn't familiar with it.

"I'm Sheriff Wegman, young lady, and I hope you've learned not to go out into the desert alone without telling anybody ever again. You got a lot of people very concerned, especially your grandparents."

It was not the congratulations for surviving that Edna had expected. Frankly she found it rude, considering what she'd just been through. People may have been concerned, but was that really important? *She* had almost died. Usually she would have pointed this out, along with the fact that it was not her "grandparents," plural, who were concerned about her, because her grandfather was practically a vegetable and hadn't been concerned about anything in years. Also, "a lot of people" depends on what you mean by "a lot." There were only about fifteen people here, at the most.

Instead, Edna took the reprimand silently. She was following her new strategy of shutting up, especially since this was happening in front of Johnny. Actually, she was hiding behind his shoulder. He didn't step away to give them any privacy, and when she thought about it later, she decided that he was protecting her.

"I won't do it ever again," Edna promised.

"It's a lot of trouble for me to round people up to go looking for somebody, and then other stuff that needs our attention, well, maybe it doesn't get it, you understand?"

"Yes. I'm sorry, sir."

"You're lucky you were found, and before dark. Plenty of people die like that. Plenty of people! Don't frighten your grandmother like that again," he reiterated as he got into his car.

"I won't, sir."

She'd already said so, but she didn't remind him of that. Edna had never used "sir" with any sincerity before. People who'd never met her before probably couldn't tell, but her mother would have detected sarcasm. In any case, Edna meant what she said, and she was not particularly proud of herself. She got off Johnny's bike.

"Don't worry about him, he has to say that stuff," Johnny told her, and he drove over to the flatbed.

Grandma did not seem at all emotional over Edna's return, in spite of how worried Johnny and Sheriff Wegman reported she had been. She told Edna to come inside for dinner. Everyone was going home now that Edna was found, not celebrating like she somehow felt they should be. A party would have been inappropriate, but at the same time Edna wished for some way to rejoice over her miraculous rescue and meeting Johnny. He drove his bike up the ramp and onto the truck. He looked strong tying it off. Edna was impressed that he did it by himself. She didn't know that many older boys.

"How did you get lost in the desert today, Edna?"

The local reporter was just doing his job, but Edna didn't appreciate the interruption of her thoughts.

"I went for a walk. I'm not from here."

"Oh, where are you from?"

"Brentwood."

"Brentwood, California?"

"Yes. L.A."

The interview continued without much of Edna's attention, as most of it was on Johnny. If she'd thought about it, she'd have known he'd leave as soon as she was safely home, but it made no sense at the moment. Johnny finished rigging his bike. Edna wandered away while the reporter was mid-question and drifted over to the flatbed. She had to have another word with Johnny. She could only think of, "Johnny, thank you."

"No worries."

She added, "Thank you, everybody."

A few of the boys waved from the cab of a truck, and one said, "We're glad you're safe." Johnny got into another truck. Moments later, tire tracks in the dirt were all that was left of the incident. It was dark and incredibly quiet.

Edna was safe from thirst and snakes and dead coyotes. She'd learned that the desert was a threatening place. Her grandparents' cabin might as well be an island she was stranded on in a treacherous ocean. She turned back to Grandma, but Grandma had already gone inside. Edna followed her. Her euphoric feeling completely evaporated once she stepped into the cabin. She noticed there were only two places set at the table.

"Is Grandpa going to eat with us?"

Grandma waved her hand to express that he would not.

"Sit down, Edna."

Edna had been on an emotional roller coaster all day, but she'd just have to hang on a little longer for whatever Grandma had in store. Bracing herself, she kept in mind that she had a lot to be grateful for recently, like meeting Johnny, drinking water and not being dead, and she added the fact that dinner was not Spam to that list. Grandma sat across from her and said a barely audible prayer. Edna just sat there and waited. She was starving.

"I don't know what this stubbornness of yours is all about," Grandma told Edna, then she went silent and started eating.

Grandma didn't say anything else. Given that Edna had ripped up Grandma's list, run away and the police had to be called, Edna was expecting some kind of lengthy lecture peppered with examples of others who'd gotten lost in the desert and died. But Grandma just looked at her plate and ate her vegetables and ham. Not being "spoken to" was nice, if bizarre. Edna couldn't wrap her mind around it. If there wasn't going to be a lecture, then polite conversation during a meal was mandatory. And yet so much time passed since Grandma's one uttered phrase, there was no denying it: that was all Grandma was going to say.

Got it, Grandma. You do not know what my stubbornness is all about.

It became a more interesting statement when Edna repeated it in her head, because she didn't really know what it was all about either.

7
EXILE

Edna decided against any further attempts at ending her life, though the suffering might be great. "I'm going to kill myself!" was a terrible figure of speech, and from now on it was as bad as profanity. Edna had learned from getting lost in the desert: No matter how dire things seem, they could always improve, so you might as well stick around. You never know when someone might drive up on a dirt bike.

But life at the cabin was challenging, even armed with a new philosophy. Edna faced empty stretches of time, broken up mostly by silent meals and reading stories about pioneer women before going to sleep. It hadn't been made quite clear to Edna that her grandmother never went anywhere, even though those were the exact words her mother had used. "Never going anywhere" to Edna still meant going to school every day and to all kinds of activities, lessons, doctors' appointments and shopping. She had no model in her life for "never going anywhere" as literally as it was meant in Grandma's case. Grandma just ate and slept with Grandpa as the sun went up and down.

She felt guilty for not at least calling Brit, but if people were having a good time, Edna didn't want to know about it. She didn't want to talk to anyone, and definitely not on Grandma's landline. She was still new at her school; people would think she was weird. Everyone else's grandparents were on Instagram. Edna couldn't say anything about her grandparents' cabin or explain why she was stuck there. The cabin wasn't even in a town; it was in an unincorporated territory ineptly named "Dream Valley." Edna thought this must have been some kind of joke, unless it referred to the fact that you'd hope you were only dreaming if you were there. It was more likely a nightmare. The whole situation was better cloaked in mystery, and that's how Edna decided to leave it.

Daydreaming was the best thing to do in Dream Valley, and Edna did it a lot. Mostly she daydreamed about Johnny: what his house was like, what he ate, if he was riding his dirt bike and if he ever thought about her. In what Edna referred to as "the real world," she would have already friended Johnny on every possible platform and found out everything about him online. She'd be able to see pictures of him and what his friends looked like. If he said where he was going, she might be able to go there too and see him again. Stripped of any electronic means of investigation and living on the edge of nowhere, Edna was powerless to create any such coincidence or even message him, if she dared. She had no idea what girls did in past centuries when they liked a boy.

Unstructured time was foreign to Edna, and she sat on the porch, giving herself assignments like counting how many live scrub brushes she could see, as opposed to how many dead ones. Johnny was right: there were a lot of dead things in the desert. She'd never noticed that before. She thought about how the tall eucalyptus trees could only live by the cabin because where people lived, there was more water in the ground. Otherwise, Joshua trees were the only things around you'd consider a tree. They were scarce and short, as trees go. Their green spikes sprouted out in all directions, and they were more like little swords than leaves. Joshua trees were whimsical, but at the same time sad to Edna, who missed the kind of towering trees she was used to. A chubby cousin of the Joshua tree was the Yucca. Hedgehog and beavertail cactus looked like their names. Grandma had some in her garden of rocky paths surrounded by chicken wire. The creosote bushes added patches of green to the sandy flatness all around. The dry air felt clean. Edna liked that.

This was the first time she was aware of having a relationship with a place and not a person. The desert, it turns out, has a will of its own and actively tries to turn everything in it into more desert by sucking it dry, sanding it down, bleaching it beige and blowing it away in the wind. It was like her vomit flaking off on the side of the road but on an infinitely larger scale, smoothing out the rolling hills in the distance as well as drying out Edna's face and hands. Edna didn't realize it at the time, but she'd abandoned any strategy to escape this aggressive landscape the moment she saw Johnny. She couldn't believe she'd stay in Grandma's cabin in the hopes of getting another glimpse of a boy, with the knowledge that she'd be bored, that she'd have to do chores and they'd be hard. The whole thing was crazy. There was no other way to describe it.

When she made it back to the real world, she'd describe her summer as a spiritual retreat, even if her mother didn't blog about it. If something couldn't be validated online, it was almost as if it never happened, but Edna thought spirituality might be an exception to this rule. In any case, spiritual retreats were popular, and everyone she knew called themselves spiritual, no matter what they believed in or how badly they behaved. Once it was over, if she presented this summer the right way, people might actually be jealous. Being spiritual for the purpose of making others jealous was not exactly the noblest reason, but Edna had no other reason at the moment. It was just that and fighting boredom.

So, she imagined she was a Tibetan monk from the documentary, and without straining to evaporate this time, she challenged herself to sit still for as long as possible. She had no idea why monks did this or if it was any different than what Grandpa did. She brought a chair out to the eucalyptus trees because she thought she remembered that the Buddha sat under a tree, but she had to keep moving to stay in the shade. It broke her concentration. It wasn't the only thing breaking it. Edna's body may have been in a chair, but her mind never sat still. She was constantly dreading her circumstances and wishing they would change instead of peacefully reaching nirvana. She tried to remember that time was passing and no matter what, the summer would eventually end, but she couldn't really believe it, and she sunk into panic attacks. Soon she learned that even within a panic attack, nothing was going to happen around here. She eventually got bored of her panic attacks along with everything else. The only other thing to do, besides freak out, was chores.

Fortunately chores, according to Grandma's rules, were self-assigned. The main chore was sweeping-everywhere-all-the-time. It wasn't fun but it was easy, and if there was any doubt as to whether she should be doing something, Edna could rely on the fact that there was always sand to pick up. Five minutes after she swept it, there it was again. She could lounge on the ugly couch daydreaming about Johnny and then spring into action if she heard Grandma coming. When Edna appeared "productive," Grandma's stern gaze slightly softened. It could be minutes or hours between Grandma's comings and goings, and sometimes Edna fell asleep in the middle of the day. If Grandma noticed, she never said anything. Edna was completely in the dark about Grandma. She had no idea why she preferred a girl to be sweeping rather than reading, or if it was just that she preferred it for Edna.

Between chores and daydreaming, Edna spent time gazing into the fridge while trying to think of things to do. It was an absentminded habit that was tolerated at home, as her father also indulged in it excessively. Grandma had fruits, vegetables, milk and meat. Her fridge was so uninteresting; it had nothing from an amazing deli and no exotic condiments.

"Are you crazy? You're letting the ice melt," Grandma said, discovering Edna immersed in fridge gazing one morning. "Ice has to last. Groceries only come once a week."

The refrigerator looked normal, if extremely old, but it was actually an icebox and not electric. In the heat of the desert, their food staying cold depended on a block of melting ice. Her grandparents' lifestyle was more like camping than Edna had guessed and probably more than her parents knew. Her mother would never have agreed to leave her there if she knew there was no refrigeration. Jill was terrified of salmonella.

When the phone rang later, Edna was sure it was one of her parents calling, because her grandparents' phone never rang. As far as Edna was concerned, she wasn't on speaking terms with those monsters, but she picked up the phone anyway. Nothing had happened that day after she was yelled at for looking in the fridge.

"Hello...Mom?"

Her father's voice put a lump in her throat. It was annoying that her emotions were so strong lately. Determined to make her parents feel terrible about leaving her there, Edna was conflicted. She had to complain, but if she made too good a case against the cabin, they might change their minds and come get her. She might never see Johnny again. She had no idea if she would anyway. Edna had no idea what she was doing.

"It's Edna."

"Hi honey, how's the summer so far?"

Edna expressed concern over the fact that she'd been left in "a slave labor camp" with "no refrigeration" and "no running water," referring to Grandma and Grandpa's water that sat in a tank next to their house. She obsessed about what would happen if the water ran out.

"You don't sit idly by while water runs out, Edna. It gets delivered," her father informed her. Edna tried to come up with more things to scare him, like "There are no doctors around here. What if I get hurt?" and "I don't think Grandma can drive."

"She can."

"What if the car doesn't start...and then the phone goes out? The service comes from a cord that runs on poles. It could break. A bird could peck at it."

Edna didn't mention that she'd put herself at greater risk than any of these possibilities by wandering out into the desert, but Edward saw no point in bringing that up or letting on that he knew about it. He replied to all her concerns with variations of "Edna, that's not going to happen." He could have a helicopter out there in ten minutes if he wanted, but he let her think she was stranded.

"Did you grow up in this shack?"

"That's not nice, and no, we lived in a house in San Diego. Grandma and Grandpa like it out there."

"You realize I'm only thirteen. I think this is against the law."

"I don't think it's against the law for you to stay with your grandparents for the summer."

It was enough to put an end to the subject. Edward hated to do this, but he'd had enough of Edna the way she was. She cried as a last resort, and she was mad at herself for it later. Her performance didn't make a dent in her father's hardened heart. She always got lost in the drama, determined to get her own way. She wanted to know that she could go home if she really tried, that she could win, but Edna wasn't getting much of what she wanted lately.

8
THE LIFE THAT GRANDMA & GRANDPA LED

Grandma always woke up before sunrise and brewed coffee. The luscious smell would seep into the pantry. Edna loved the smell of coffee, but she hated the taste of it. She listened to Grandma move around her strangely improvised home. At least Edna thought it was strange. A washer/dryer and an electric stove stood outside the cabin, on a cement slab under a lean-to of green, corrugated plastic. It was enclosed by stacked driftwood. It was just a little too funky to be nice. There wasn't much space in the cabin, Edna guessed, and maybe Grandma cooked outside in the summer, when it was too hot to have the stove on inside. Observing the Grandma and Grandpa situation more closely, Edna realized that the pantry was the most private place Grandma could have offered her to sleep and might not have been the additional punishment it seemed when she'd first arrived.

Edna could never fall back to sleep once she woke up in the morning, so she turned on her little lamp and read before Grandma knocked on the door and said, "breakfast." Books about pioneer women were Edna's only entertainment, and her parents' hint was not so subtle: these women struggled on a level that should shame Edna into being grateful for her life of relative ease. Edna *was* grateful, but at the moment it was mainly for the distraction of these incredible stories. Many of the pioneer women left privileged lives to trek across mountains, rivers and deserts, in horse-driven carriages or on foot, to help their husbands look for gold and homestead. After her own brief drama in the wilderness, Edna was awed by the strength it took to survive this. These women, some not much older than she was, had passions and abilities she didn't fully understand. She might possess a shadow of their fortitude by sacrificing her entire summer in the hopes of getting to see a boy again, but that was just crazy more than anything else.

After coffee was made, Grandma would bring a mug to Grandpa, who presumably drank it in bed. Edna never saw this happen. She was revolted by the thought of her grandparents in bed, and she kept completely clear of their bedroom. Grandma said that Grandpa liked his eggs "just so," and she was very attentive while she boiled them so they would be perfect every time. It was something that Grandpa must have told her years ago, but Edna doubted that he noticed now. She couldn't imagine her grandparents as a young couple that did things together and spoke to each other. Grandma brought Grandpa's breakfast, two eggs and toast, into the bedroom on a tray every morning, and he also had that in bed. Grandma didn't eat breakfast, but she made scrambled egg whites and toast for Edna. Grandma was stingy with her affection, but she was not stingy about feeding people.

About two hours after breakfast, Grandpa would emerge from the bedroom, silent as always. It was one of the few times he moved. He wore a T-shirt and flannel pajama pants. Edna was happy to never see too much of his old body. He went directly into the bathroom and didn't come out for at least an hour, when Grandma brought him his clothes. Grandpa came out dressed, walked to the porch and sat in the old wooden office chair with a formerly orange cushion on it. He spent the majority of each day there while Grandma went about maintaining their food, clothing and shelter.

Grandpa's lunch was leftovers from yesterday's dinner, or if nothing was left over, it was Spam or canned hash. Grandma brought it to him on a rusted TV tray with purple flowers that leaned against the railing. Grandpa didn't express anything, ever, except he did seem to love hash. Edna believed this was love because he ate it fast, with an uncivilized snorting sound. Watching Grandpa eat was not unlike watching an animal in a zoo, and like zoo animals, he could get annoyed. Edna got a little too curious for him one day, which he indicated by becoming conscious, raising his eyebrow and peering right at her. Edna shrieked and almost bounced out of her chair.

When Grandma rushed out, Edna thought this must have been the concerned look that Johnny and Sheriff Wegman saw the day she was lost. Grandpa was already back in his catatonic state as if nothing had happened.

"Grandpa looked at me."

"Oh."

Grandma peered at Grandpa for a moment and then went back to whatever she was doing. Edna thought she'd be more interested in a lucid appearance by Grandpa. The world became inactive again, too quiet. It was moments like that, when it was quiet after something happened, that felt frighteningly still in the desert.

Edna started to observe things in this place where almost nothing happened, and she attributed her heightened awareness to the media blackout she lived in. Her mind thirsted for new facts. Sometimes a certain cactus would bend over one way and then be in a different position a few hours later. Edna tried, but she could never see it move. A scrub brush looked different degrees of dead from morning to afternoon, or was the color changing with the movement of the sun? An old wildlife guide she found in the garage offered no explanation. Spotting quail or a jackrabbit was entertainment, as Edna looked after the animals and wondered where they lived, what they ate and what in the world they drank. The guide had pictures, a few sentences and practically no information. She wished she knew what had happened to that little bunny she saw when she was lost, but there were some things that were impossible to know, even if your phone had service.

Edna moved a chair out to the porch one afternoon as something new to try: Sitting with Grandpa. She didn't know why she was afraid of him, he seemed harmless. Grandma had explicitly written "don't bother Grandpa" on that list Edna had torn up. Was sitting next to him bothering him? Grandpa's eyes were dull, he didn't seem to notice her. His only movement was the gentle rising and falling of his chest under his flannel shirt. Some gray hairs stuck out of the top of it. It was too hot for flannel, but Grandpa was so still all the time, maybe he didn't get hot. Or maybe he was boiling but unable to say so. Edna doubted that, he wasn't sweating. The breeze lifted little hairs on his arms. His face looked like Edna's father's would if a sculptor chiseled deeper definition into it and a painter grayed his hair and roughed his skin. As far as Edna could tell, Grandpa's head was an empty shell.

She challenged herself to empty her own head, but she sighed and fidgeted. Her thoughts drifted to Johnny and things like the sweat that came through his T-shirt. For some reason his sweat wasn't gross. She wondered if he ever thought about her. She wondered what he was having for dinner and then what Grandma would make for dinner and if Grandpa ever cared what she made. She didn't understand how Grandpa was able to do some things, like put food on a fork and put it in his mouth, but not others, like help Grandma do anything, or talk. She didn't even know if Grandpa saw the expansive landscape in front of them the same way she did.

There was no homework, no French or piano to practice, no gymnastics or yoga or debate team. Why was being good at all these things so important anyway? Edna had no parties to go to and no gifts to buy. She was missing some birthdays. She didn't have a million texts to return, and she didn't have to load a bunch of photos and write captions for them. Or tweet or retweet. She had no way to Pin. She had no idea what was going on on Snapchat or Instagram and her Tumblr hadn't been updated in ages. It was irritating that her profiles were out there with no way of hiding how abruptly they'd been abandoned.

In the real world, Edna was always doing something and then posting about it. Her rhythm of changing activities every hour, every day, was slowly unraveling here in the desert, with no next activity and no audience to look to for constant encouragement. She painted the porch for four hours one day, which she only estimated because of the cramp in her shoulder and the changed position of the sun, and no one but Grandma knew about it.

Because of their rocky start, Edna kept a polite distance from Grandma most of the time. This was easy, as Grandma spent chunks of her days crocheting or absorbed in her cactus garden which was was far enough from the cabin, Edna thought, to make Grandma feel like she went somewhere. She'd created an extensive, unpredictable network of stone-lined paths that wound around quirky tableaus of mature cactus, ornamental rocks and cement garden gnomes. It must have taken years. When Edna asked if she could help her with it, Grandma only shrugged and seemed confused.

"I make it up as I go along."

Edna soon understood that the garden was Grandma's creative project, one she was not trying to finish. This was a new concept. The constant expectation of finishing things, of setting goals and achieving them, was already deeply rooted in Edna, but her mental habit struggled with nothing to do in the middle of nowhere. Edna started her own projects, like painting the porch and making a stone path from the cabin to the eucalyptus trees. Looking for large, flat rocks was a great way to waste time.

If anything was a sin in the real world, it was wasting time, but at the cabin that was all she did, and she could see how a person could get used to it. Maybe the real world was too hectic. She'd become much more likely to snap than she used to be. Her therapist should have thought of this a long time ago. It was decided: the first thing Edna would cut out of her routine when she got home would be therapy sessions. Talking about everything did not always help. Sometimes Edna was sure that not talking about things would be better, but then she was accused of "avoiding" and told she needed more therapy.

The sun was getting low, and Edna had done tons of chores to keep from being bored. Doing nothing felt like falling—out of what and into what she didn't know, but every afternoon it took a while before she stopped trying to think of things to do. All the laundry was folded. There was no point in sweeping any more. There were no more dishes until after dinner. She'd already been a Tibetan monk three times that day, and even though that literally meant doing nothing, she just couldn't do it anymore.

Grandma would make dinner soon. She was tired of checking on Edna by that point, so sitting with Grandpa in the late afternoon was the best part of Edna's day. The wind picked up by then and became an invisible beach ball tumbling across the sea of creosote bushes and wafting over their smoky smell. The long afternoon shadows swayed in a rhythm that calmed Edna, and the breeze cooled her. If she'd had been told a week ago that the best part of her day would be sitting next to Grandpa on the porch staring into the desert, she definitely would not have believed it.

Edna also wouldn't have guessed that she'd miss the nightly dinnertime interrogations from her mother and the constantly fidgeting mess of Brandon. Dinner was terrible here, offering unfamiliar foods that were high in sodium. It created an interaction with Grandma unbuffered by chores or logistics. Edna was discovering new things about herself in exile, and one of them was that she didn't like being alone with a person who never had anything to say, if that person was capable of talking. Grandpa had an excuse, though Edna wasn't sure what it was, and she liked being around him better. She hated being around Grandma. Grandma's silence felt like rejection, and Edna's comments that "it was a beautiful day," "I saw a jackrabbit" or "I might paint the porch" were given a word or two back and then, instead of being nurtured into a conversation, were left to wither. Edna thought about making up a tray and eating outside with Grandpa, but by the time dinner rolled around, sitting with Grandpa was not exactly something worth fighting for. It was hard to eat with such a big lump in her throat, but soon Edna got used to it, and then it went away. Her mother's incessant questioning would be forever less irritating. It had only been six days, but watching her family drive away in the Audi felt like a hundred years ago.

9
DELIVERY

Edna decided to acquire a taste for coffee as another thing to do for the summer. She found it bitter and absolutely hideous, but celebrities were always pictured with a coffee in their hands, and she wanted to know why. It was tolerable if she put enough sugar in it. She couldn't believe this was what adults craved every morning, and it gave her all the more reason to question authority in the future. Edna stepped onto the porch with her mug for the first time of the day. She would probably step onto the porch fifty more times throughout the day before her late-afternoon sitting session with Grandpa. The only thing that ever changed much was the angle of the sun and the occasional lean of a cactus.

But this morning a line of dust rose in the distance, which meant a vehicle was coming. The dust moved north along the ridge until it turned and made its way east. It was coming toward the cabin. Edna guessed it was her parents. Maybe this was still a trick! Instead of the whole summer, it was only going to be a week. As the vehicle got closer, Edna could see it was a little red pick-up truck with a cap on the back. Did her parents buy a truck? On the side it said *Bishop's General*. She wasn't even sure it was coming to the cabin, though she couldn't think of where else it could be going.

Edna wished it could be Johnny driving the truck. She tried to convince herself that it was too ridiculous a thing to hope for, but her heart beat rapidly as if it knew otherwise. Because it did. It was him. Johnny was driving the truck, which could only be coming to the cabin. Edna got dizzy for a moment as this sunk in. Her hand forgot about the mug of coffee it was holding and spilled it. The coffee wasn't hot enough to burn her, but it left her chest covered in an ugly splotch. Emergency. She dashed into the pantry. She emptied her drawers until she found her cutest pink T-shirt at the bottom of one of them. It was tapered and made her look like she had curves. She brushed back her

47

strawberry hair, a horrible, unwashed mess. There was no time to do anything about it, so she threw it in a ponytail.

When Edna's friends had started liking boys a year or two before, she had been determined not to allow it to happen to her. Girls acted like idiots when they liked boys. How to say "hi" to a boy in school became a stupid preoccupation, considering which hallway to walk down and how many seconds after the bell. It was always a waste of time. Even if Brit liked a boy and got to kiss him, they broke up in a few weeks and each started on the next, most popular person they had a chance with. Edna didn't want to like boys, or girls, which would have been fine, or so the adults around her went to great lengths to make clear. Edna didn't want to like anyone, but it was already well underway. She'd just spilled coffee and thrown her clothes all over the place in less than a minute.

When she got back to the porch, the red truck was parked. Johnny approached the cabin with bags of groceries in his arms. It was magical, impossible: he was even cuter than she remembered. He wasn't dusty this time. There was something energetic and graceful about the way he moved. His hair was wild. Boys at Edna's school put tons of gel in their hair to get it to look like that, and they never succeeded. He said, "Hi Edna," as if it was the most natural thing in the world.

"Hi," Edna eked out.

"Staying out of trouble, I hope."

Before she could respond, he went inside. Edna felt somehow special because Johnny knew her name and because he hoped she was not in trouble. She was lightheaded again. She watched as he helped Grandma unpack the bags. He seemed to know his way around Grandma's kitchen. Edna couldn't believe it was all happening. When he took some cans to the pantry, she was so hypnotized she forgot she'd left her clothes, including her underwear, scattered all over the place.

"I was doing laundry," she yelped as she dashed ahead of him, gathering the more humiliating items first.

"Sorry, Edna, I didn't know this is your room now."

There was no irony, sarcasm or anything in his voice that would indicate an opinion of the fact that Edna was sleeping in the pantry or hanging her laundry all over it. He put down the cans. Edna dropped her clothes and followed him out. She could smell his T-shirt again, this one navy blue. In the big room Johnny gave Grandma some mail, and Grandma gave Johnny some bills. He told her he'd check the car.

It hadn't occurred to Edna that Grandma might know Johnny, but apparently he delivered her groceries and mail, and he maintained her car. Anyone else might have mentioned it.

Edna peered around the side of the cabin and watched Johnny open the garage door. He lifted the hood of Grandma and Grandpa's Bronco, took something out, a stick, and wiped it off with a rag. Edna guessed he was checking the oil. She was impressed; she didn't know men who knew anything about cars. Men she knew brought them in for repairs and had expensive tool sets at home that were unused.

Johnny started the Bronco and drove away, leaving Edna in one of those desert quiets that came after something big happened. If the red truck wasn't right in front of her, Edna might doubt that Johnny had been there at all. She could have easily hallucinated the whole scene out of boredom.

She regretted going to the garage to wait for him moments later. She was awkward and inauthentic among the rusty tools and ancient engine parts that lay exactly where they had hit the ground however many years ago. The remains of her grandparents' lives, their dusty furniture and memories, were neglected here and dominated the space, except for where the Bronco parked. Edna couldn't imagine a good reason to be standing here, weirdly in wait for Johnny. She was about to leave, but she heard the Bronco coming up the sandy road. Walking away would seem cold. This boy just saved her life; she couldn't exactly ignore him. She did her best to start organizing

Grandpa's old tools with a sense of purpose while he parked and got out.

"Where did you go off to?"

Off too? That sounded forced.

"Down the road. You have to move a car once in a while if you want to keep it running."

"Uh-huh."

Edna couldn't think of a thing to add to this.

"See you next week," he said, and he went back to the truck.

Edna froze, then followed him. She'd lost any ability to monitor herself and stared after him like a puppy left behind. He got into the truck and waved as he drove off. She waved back. Her heart sank as the truck sped away, but it buoyed again when the brake lights went on. Johnny backed the truck up and got out.

"I forgot to give you this. You're famous."

He handed her a copy of *The Desert Weekly* with a picture of the two of them on Johnny's dirt bike. It was on the front page.

"Oh. Thank you."

"No problem."

He smiled and went back to the truck. Edna loved to watch him walk. She didn't look down at the newspaper or even blink until the red truck was out of sight.

The newspaper's headline read *Girl Found Safely in Dream Valley,* confirming that absolutely nothing went on around here if this was a top story. The picture was of two helmeted and therefore expressionless people. Edna reflected that if Johnny were not wearing a helmet, she might have a nice picture of him, but she thanked God she was wearing one. She had been shocked at how awful she looked when she finally saw a mirror that night. The flash blew out any detail in Johnny's white T-shirt, so the shape of his body was indiscernible. It was a terrible photo by any standard, but it was of the two of them, and Edna would keep it forever. She wondered if Johnny would keep one. Probably not. She learned that his last name was Bishop, which was the same as the store he'd delivered the groceries from. He lived in Desert Palms, and he was on the Dirt Bike Response Crew for Search and Rescue, confirming that he was a good person who cared about his community. He was seventeen.

Edna knew he was older, but she was intimidated by that number. She would have felt better if he was fifteen or even sixteen, but she didn't know why it made such a difference.

10
PINEAPPLE UPSIDE-DOWN CAKE

Edna would never admit it to her parents, but the pioneer women she read about every evening blew her mind. The logistics of their migrations across the country in the mid-1800s ranged from arduous to impossible. These young women often made the trip alone or with children in covered wagons pulled by oxen, traveling thousands of miles at a pace of ten miles a day. Some traveled on foot, pushing handcarts that carried the only supplies they'd have for many months. Edna couldn't imagine the afternoon she was lost in the desert going on for any longer than it did, let alone having to push a heavy cart in the dirt for thousands of miles, cooking and feeding children while doing it and tending to oxen in all kinds of weather. She might as likely think she could walk to the moon.

Her favorite pioneer was Mrs. Anderson. At nineteen years old, she had already become a "Mrs." and she and her husband provided a window into history because they saved their letters in a metal box. The letters were found and eventually published. Edna thought it would be romantic if their lives hadn't been so difficult. Mr. Anderson had gone West years (yes, years) before Mrs. Anderson in search of gold. He finally found some and could afford for her to join him. A photograph of his handwritten letter was in a sidebar of one of the books, which were all a little too textbook-like to get completely lost in. In any case, Mrs. Anderson's trip, one she would make across the continent in a covered wagon, was two thousand miles. The list of things to do for the trip was extensive, including engineering a way to haul an eighty-pound sack of flour and keeping writing paper safe and dry from Kentucky to California. There were nearly a hundred tasks on the list. Edna wasn't sure if it was outrageous that a young woman be expected to acquire and pack so many things for such a rugged journey or if this was normal and expected. If it was normal and expected, Edna was glad she was alive now instead of then. Getting lost and sleeping in Grandma's pantry was rugged enough, and Edna wasn't sure any amount of gold could change that. Although being with Johnny might. Edna imagined that most of the pioneer women didn't make the trip for gold, but for love. Nothing else could explain it. Grandma had a lot in common with these pioneer women. Her whole life was like being on a cross-country wagon trail, except she never went anywhere.

Edna dozed off reading the Andersons' letters, until she was disturbed by pans rattling around the shelves above her cot. The cabin shook. An earthquake. In the big room, Grandma's rainbow crochet pillows bounced around her ugly couch. Edna stepped onto the porch. She must have overslept because the sun was high and strong. It was hard to keep her footing with the sudden, jerking motions. The cabin was moving under her, but strangely, it wasn't an earthquake after all. Or maybe the earthquake was over. The cabin cut through a choppy sea, and the distant hills moved past at a clip. The cool ocean wind was heaven. Ahead, blue oxen charged through water up to their shoulders, pulling chains attached to the cabin. Grandma commanded all three of them on a leash. Grandpa stayed in his chair as usual, though it tipped back and forth as the porch hit rough water. He fell too far back, and Edna rushed to him, but she was distracted by a shark's fin breaking through the water's surface. When she turned around for Grandpa, he was gone. So was his chair. She had no time to figure out where he went because the shark's fin emerged from the water as Johnny, speeding along the porch on his dirt bike, dust kicking up behind him. Edna waved, but he didn't notice her. The porch seemed longer than it could be as she ran, keeping pace with him. He veered away from the cabin, and Edna tried, like a Hollywood stuntman, to jump from the railing onto his bike. She soared, confident she could make it, but she missed and was left choking in dust.

Edna woke up spitting flour out of her mouth. A sack sat on the floor, most of its contents on her head and pillow. A mouse rummaging the shelves must have knocked it over. The little guy cowered and escaped. If anyone saw a mouse at home, Jill would call the exterminator and they would all go to a hotel for a few days, but here no one was going to do anything about it. Edna swept the floor and changed her sheets.

She still had a flour in her hair when she stepped onto the porch. It was the time of night it was supposed to be, though it was nearly bright enough to read a book. The full moon cast shadows that were almost as hard as the sun's and displayed a different desert, with a palette of dark greens, browns, and blacks. Night had an even more profound stillness, and Edna let it seep into her as she sat in her chair. There was no chance of falling asleep again.

She was glad her embarrassing jump off the porch wasn't real. She'd try to have a better dream about Johnny next time. She'd try not to throw herself at him or imagine he was so far away and totally unattainable. He had said "see you next week," hadn't he? Edna thought so, but she couldn't be completely sure she had heard right. His back had been to her, and he had been walking toward the truck.

In any case, Edna couldn't wait an entire week to see Johnny again. So far she'd given 100% of what was required of her; she shouldn't be held at the cabin like a prisoner. Nothing outlined in the rules of this punishment should conflict with a trip to a store, if Grandma really could drive. Why shouldn't she and Grandma go out? The plan was to get Grandma to take her to Bishop's General, even though Grandma had everything she thought she needed brought to her.

A good way to get her mother to go out was to create a need for baking ingredients. Jill loved doing anything domestic because she could blog about it, so Edna would find recipes for desserts with obscure ingredients and then suggest a shopping trip. On the way, Edna would mention what she really wanted in the first place as if it were an afterthought. If Jill was as distracted as she usually was, Edna could convince her to stop for a phone upgrade or new jeans. It was just so much faster to upgrade a phone than to fight with Edna.

The major downside of the plot was having to do research and actually make desserts, otherwise it wouldn't work the next time. And Edna hated being a recurring character in videos on Shimmer, but that part mattered less and less. No one remembered anything about anyone's videos anymore unless they were famous or the videos had sex in them. The other downside was that Edna was becoming a dessert expert, and Jill was so happy about it. Edna would never be able to tell her mother that it was all an act. Baking had become a permanent part of her personality, and Edna had no idea how to stop it.

She found a cookbook in Grandma's pantry. It had sat in the same spot for years, evident from the mark left on the shelf when Edna took it down that evening. She liked the cracking sound that the book's dried out spine made when she opened it, and she loved the faded paper's smell.

Edna had already decided to make her father's favorite dessert, Pineapple Upside-Down Cake, an esoteric offering that Grandma was unlikely to have all the ingredients for. She was going to give the cake to Johnny eventually, so it had to be something out of this world. Edna knew she could make a good one. She didn't need a recipe; she'd made it with her mother a hundred times. The recipe was a visual aid in getting her trip to the store for ingredients. Better it was written in a book and not just on her say-so. Edna was confident in her plan to get to Bishop's. A girl baking a cake was the most natural thing in the world.

She turned to the recipe for Pineapple Upside-Down Cake, and a yellowed clipping that was saved there floated to the floor. It was from a newspaper called The *San Diego Gazette* and dated September 16, 1964. The headline said: SAN DIEGO SWEETIE TAKES TOP PINEAPPLE PRIZE. Grandma, practically unrecognizable as a young woman named Mary Miller, had won a blue ribbon for what was described as her "knock-out delicious" Pineapple Upside-Down Cake. The article went on to say that Mrs. Miller was the wife of Lt. Ezekiel Miller, a Marine serving in Vietnam. Mary smiled sweetly behind her creation, the most robust Pineapple Upside-Down Cake that Edna had ever seen. Each pineapple ring was bursting with clusters of cherries and surrounded by flowers of chopped walnuts. The details were shown, but they were grainy in the old newspaper's close-ups.

What felt like an uncanny coincidence was, in fact, no coincidence at all. Edna had thought of making Pineapple Upside-Down Cake because her father loved it, only she never knew that he loved it because his mother, this stranger named Mary Miller, made the best one in San Diego County in 1964.

The page where the clipping was kept read: *Pineapple Upside-Down Cake, a recipe by Mary Miller of San Diego, California.* Grandma was published.

For the first time Edna understood that her life was probably influenced in many ways by Mary Miller, and that her grandmother was a real person who had done more than subsist in this depressing desert all her life. It was an obvious point. It shouldn't have surprised her, but it came as quite a shock. She had trouble sleeping that night, trying to picture her young grandmother. Nothing she came up with fit the person she knew.

The next morning, Edna brought her new curiosity about her grandparents and the cookbook into the kitchen. She'd never really tried being friendly to Grandma before. She'd been too devastated after being abandoned here to think about being nice. This morning, friendliness was the plan. She sincerely wanted to get to know Grandma better, but she had to be careful. It could look suspicious if she was suddenly too cheerful, as if she had an ulterior motive—which, even with her new interest, she did.

Grandma didn't say anything about the cookbook Edna held when she came out of the pantry. Any other adult in her life would have said something if she walked into a room with a book, something like, "What are you reading?" In that case she would have told Grandma about how she found this book in the pantry and how she really loved making desserts. She'd talk about a few different recipes before even mentioning that they should a bake a cake, or which one. She would pretend they were picking out a recipe together. Edna was good at manipulating most of the adults she knew and harnessing their need to be liked by children, but she was still making too many assumptions about Grandma based on her other life.

"So, today, Grandma, I was thinking…I was feeling homesick, and I…"

Grandma didn't soften her expression at Edna's mention of being homesick.

"Sometimes, at home, I bake cakes or cookies with Mom, and Dad eats them mostly, but I was wondering if we could bake something and if you liked cake at all…or if Grandpa does."

Did that make sense? Edna waited as though it was perfectly normal for Grandma to take so long to think about baking a cake.

"I guess we could."

Normally Edna would smile and there would be a bonding moment, but there was no point in pushing for that. Edna opened the cookbook. She told Grandma how she hadn't been this happy about baking a cake in a long time and that it was going to be fun. She didn't have the patience to go through her usual twists before getting to the Pineapple Upside-Down Cake; it would probably be wasted on Grandma anyway. Edna was intrigued by what made Grandma tick, but she was way more interested in trying to get to Bishop's.

"I read somewhere that you're an expert at my favorite cake, which is Pineapple Upside-Down," she announced.

She took out the old newspaper clipping and held it for Grandma to see. Grandma took it. Her hand went over her mouth, and her eyes welled up with tears. Without a word she went into the bedroom.

It was not the reaction Edna was expecting. She'd planned for Grandma to be tickled by her interest. Seeing the old article and Edna's improved friendliness, Grandma would drop everything and tell her all about winning the first-prize ribbon at the San Diego County Fair. Then they would go shopping for Pineapple Upside-Down Cake ingredients and see Johnny, and Edna hadn't even begun to imagine how amazing that was going to be.

Instead, Edna sat alone in one of those long desert silences while she tried to figure out what had just happened. Grandma seemed truly upset. Edna was pretty sure she hadn't done anything wrong, but she felt guilty.

She was tempted to call home and ask her father if some horrible incident occurred involving Pineapple Upside-Down Cake or the San Diego County Fair. She might ask her mother what to do about a crying grandmother you didn't really know all that well. But Edna reminded herself that she didn't want to give those tyrants the satisfaction of helping her and that she'd hoped to go the rest of the summer without speaking to them. Getting a trip to the store might be more difficult than she'd thought, for reasons she didn't even know existed. Concerned and not sure what to do next, Edna didn't know if Grandma was all right. She wanted to apologize, if only for bringing up something that made her react so strongly. Edna listened at the door. If Grandma was crying in the bedroom, she was doing it quietly. Grandpa, in there with her, was silent as usual.

Edna gently tapped the door. Even if Grandma said, "Go away," at least she would know that Edna cared about her. A few moments passed, but Grandma didn't come and there wasn't any sound. Edna knocked again, trying to sound a little louder but even kinder than before. Again, no answer. There was nothing to do. Edna swept the porch hoping that Grandma would come out. In a few minutes, she did. She went directly to the phone. Edna watched through an open window, too curious to interrupt her.

Grandma looked up a number on a handwritten list and dialed it, a few numbers at a time. She spoke into the phone like it was a foreign object.

"Hello, is that Jenny? This is Mary Miller. Will you please add, uh...four cans of Dole pineapples, the sliced rings in juice, two fresh pineapples, a pound of butter, a pound of white flour, a bag of walnuts, and, uh, two jars of maraschino cherries and a pound and a half of fresh cherries. Add that to my order next week, please. Thank you."

She hung up the phone and set up Grandpa's breakfast like she always did. She looked fine. Another silence. Grandma was standing exactly where she had been, doing the same exact thing as before she went into the bedroom. Edna wondered if Grandma knew the ingredients for Pineapple Upside-Down Cake by heart, or maybe she was looking them up. Grandma's reaction to the newspaper clipping was still a mystery, but Edna saw a bigger issue emerging: the next grocery order would be coming next week—that was, in five days. The entire point of baking a cake was that Edna was hoping to hop in the car and be off to town in a few minutes.

She leaned on the windowsill.

"Thanks, Grandma," she said, without meaning it much.

Grandma nodded, which meant, "You're welcome."

Grandma had done what she thought Edna wanted, and right away. Edna couldn't think of a good enough reason to need to bake a cake now rather than next week, and she'd read enough Shimmer to know that she should leave things the way they were. Etiquette dictates that you never get what you want, and you have to pretend you're happy with it. Etiquette meant waiting another five entire days to see Johnny, if he was the one delivering the groceries next week and it wasn't someone else. She had no idea what had happened with Grandma, but she'd think of another reason to go to town. She had all day to think of one.

While it was tempting, Edna couldn't share with Grandma why she wanted to go to Bishop's, even though Grandma might know things about Johnny. She might be able to tell Edna what his house was like, if he was smart, or what he liked to do besides dirt biking. While Grandma had become slightly more human, Edna wouldn't count her as an ally yet. She didn't want some grandmother tapping her foot while she tried to charm Johnny in the grocery store or letting on that she'd been asking questions about him. Worse, if Edna divulged her new secret about liking Johnny, Grandma could have too much power over the outcome of any number of situations involving him. She thought about what to do next while she swept for a few more minutes.

"Grandma, do you ever go to Desert Palms?"

"Not much."

"Grandma, I'd like to…see some things around here. Would you show me around town, maybe? Tomorrow? Please?"

Mary didn't exactly remember the last time she went anywhere, but it could have been about a year ago, when Zeke went to the doctor. She reflected on that day, when she'd decided he'd have no more doctor visits. Edward had agreed. He wasn't improving with any of them, not anymore.

While waiting for Grandma to answer her question, Edna wondered what Grandma's opinion of Desert Palms was, why she never went there and how she could stand this dreary life.

"I'll try the car tomorrow," Grandma said, and then she added, "It must be boring for a girl your age around here."

"Yes, a little."

Edna was relieved. Grandma finally understood something about her. Edna understood very little about Grandma.

11
TOWN

Edna put together the cutest outfit she possibly could. Her clothes, secretly packed by her mother, were too juvenile and sporty. She took out the appalling salmon dress she had been convinced to visit her grandparents in and decided to bury it in a hole later, so there'd be no chance of it coming back to Brentwood. The best look she could come up with was a fitted green vest that looked better with nothing underneath it and her jean skirt. She hated her modified ballet slippers, and sneakers were out, so she put on flip-flops. Her mother refused to let her have heels, claiming thirteen was too young wear them, even though celebrities' five-year-olds wore them in magazines. Jill had Shimmer to think about and she couldn't set a bad example, or so she always said. Every milestone in Edna's life had to be age-appropriate for the house dullards of Shimmer, and as a result, Edna could not wear a wedge or a pair of cute platforms.

Luckily she was permitted to carry her own purse, and having handled that enormous responsibility for a while, she was no longer subject to checks of what was in it every day. Edna had a little bit of makeup—eyeliner, pink lipstick and nail polish. Everyone brought makeup to school and put it on in the bathroom if they weren't allowed to wear it at home. It turned out it was better that the trip to town was delayed so she could have time to consider her outfit and do her nails. She never did her own anymore, only touch-ups. At least there was less chance of messing it up here; polish dries quickly in the desert.

Edna didn't know what kind of girls Johnny liked so she created the most grown-up, feminine look she could. Some boys swore they liked natural girls with no makeup on, but they were in the minority and Edna didn't quite believe them. She left her hair down and put one little braid on the side. She tried to convince herself that there was no certainty of seeing Johnny just because they were going to town. If she didn't run into him, she shouldn't be too disappointed. She had no way of adhering to this philosophy, but the effort might cushion the blow if that was how things turned out. As much as she tried to establish a certain maturity, Edna knew she'd be crushed if she didn't see Johnny, even though he could be out on a remote delivery, not unlike the one he made to Grandma's every week, or on any number of errands. There was only so long they could wait around at a grocery store if he was out. Maybe he didn't even work that day. Edna had no idea how they'd end up at Bishop's to begin with.

She looked perfect for popping into a grocery store; if she were any more done up she'd look like she was on her way to something formal. Around here, what could that be?

Grandma passed the window on her way to the garage. Her walk didn't have its usual authority. Edna read this as trepidation about driving. Grandma opened the garage door and got into the Bronco. She searched the dashboard for some time before she turned the car on. It pulled forward, stopped short and stalled. Grandma started it again and drove it up to the cabin. Her dress had to be ironed. She took an old pair of shoes out of the closet and cleaned them. She washed her hair and put it up. When she was dressed, she loaded two gallons of water into the Bronco. She packed apples and oranges into a cooler. Grandma's preparation for a trip to town was not unlike Mrs. Anderson's preparation for a transcontinental journey. They could have easily gone to town and back by now.

Edna waited on the porch next to Grandpa. No matter how long Grandma took, she was not going to get distracted and start doing things that might get her dirty, which was anything she could do at the cabin. At home, Jill would have told her she had too much makeup on and made her go wash her face, but when Grandma put a glass of water next to Grandpa's chair, she only glanced at Edna slightly longer than she usually might. She didn't say anything. Edna didn't know she was preoccupied with leaving Grandpa. The last time Mary had left him, she'd moved him inside, but he was outside again when she came back. She didn't bother with it today. They'd only be gone for a few hours.

Both women were oddly done up in contrast to their normal, everyday looks and the rugged surroundings. Neither of them commented on it. They got into the car and put on their seat belts. Grandma showed no signs of hesitation when she started up the Bronco and drove off. Edna was impressed with Grandma. She didn't complain about any of the effort it took for her to take this trip. It may have been because she didn't generally talk, but her mother, along with most people Edna knew, made a point of letting others know when they were going out of their way for them. They always tried to be so subtle that they could never be accused of intentionally conveying this, but there was nothing subtle about it.

The last vehicle Edna had ridden was Johnny's dirt bike, and she felt a thrill as the Bronco rumbled away from the cabin and into the rest of the world, or at least some semblance of civilization. Or a semblance of a semblance. They traveled up the road in silence, which, in this case, Edna preferred. Everything under the big, brilliant sky, every hill, scrub brush, rock and grain of sand was brimming with potential, and she wanted to be in tune with all of it.

Fifteen minutes later the Bronco stood at a traffic light, surrounded by clusters of small, beige buildings. Edna had been to the intersection before, on the way to Grandma's. She hadn't known that what she could see from the intersection was most of the town of Desert Palms. Made up of a few blocks of essential offices and stores, it had a disproportionately large number of tattoo parlors. A sign pointed to a Marine base. Distant rumblings Edna sometimes heard were bombs set off as part of their training exercises. A barbershop gave "Military Haircuts," and Chinese massage was offered in an old storefront that once displayed "Bob's Hats." Empty hat stands propped up a sun-faded sign about the benefits of massage in broken English. Everything looked run-down. There were no people. The town was gloomy, and it also seemed a little angry, even though the day was bright. Grandma pulled over.

"I don't really know what there is to see around here, Edna."

Grandma let out a little sigh. So did Edna.

"I guess I thought there might be something."

There was one thing. Moments later they were in front of a mural on the side of one of the little beige buildings. It immortalized a doctor. He was bald and wore glasses and a lab coat. It was an illustration with the kind of muted colors that might be in an old science book. The mural told the story of how the doctor treated veterans of World War I and recommended that they live in the desert if their lungs had been hurt by mustard gas. Thus he was responsible for attracting many of the few people who'd settled in the area.

"What's mustard gas?"

"It's a kind of chemical warfare."

"Did it hurt Grandpa?"

"Goodness, no. He's not that old. No one who fought in that war is still alive."

Edna didn't know when it had been.

In her travels, she'd noticed that towns that had nothing defining them often had murals in order to seem like they had something. Edna usually disliked murals. Perhaps she hadn't seen many good ones. Her judgment aside, Edna was grateful for the murals of Desert Palms. She wanted at least one thing to do before suggesting to Grandma that they go to Bishop's for a reason she hadn't thought of yet. Grandma had packed enough provisions to rule out most of the reasons she might come up with to go to a grocery store. Edna's mind raced as they stood in front of the murals and baked in the midday sun.

One mural honored Marines. Others depicted people who'd established something, like a newspaper or a church or a bus line to civilization. It didn't look like things had progressed very much in the century since these initial activities. Here these rugged folks were thanked for all eternity, or for as long as these buildings might stand, for inspiring what seemed to Edna to be a pretty depressing scene. Somehow it was even more depressing when she stood next to each mural, small and alone, while Grandma took a picture on Edna's phone.

When she had turned it on, all together there were 217 unread messages and texts. The first ten were from Brit. Edna felt a pang of guilt, but not the panic she would have felt before she'd been left in the desert. Normally, if she didn't respond to a text in a few hours, she might not remember to later. There was nothing to be done about all of these.

She didn't know if she liked the murals of Desert Palms because it was Johnny's town or if it was actually fun to see jackrabbits, quail and roadrunners supersized in colorful paint. In "Early Life at the Oasis," Native Americans huddled next to a tiny lake in a forest of palms. It was just the kind of place Edna had been hoping to die next to in the desert when she got lost on her "walk." Did it really exist? She couldn't imagine this shady, fertile setting was anywhere near such a harsh, treeless one. It was more likely a legend.

"Is this place real? Can we go to it?"

"I went there, sometime in the late nineties, I think it was."

"So it's real?"

"Oh, yes."

Grandma might have lived in vast, open spaces, but she did not get around much. It was a foreign way of existing to Edna, who was comparatively well-traveled thanks to her adventurous parents. Edna wondered aloud if they could go ask someone where the oasis was, advancing the project of getting to Bishop's. She wouldn't have all day before she was a sweaty mess, and she couldn't think of a better excuse to pop into a store. At least Grandma knew where Bishop's was. So far the day was going perfectly.

Bishop's was set back from the sidewalk, and it faded into its dull surroundings. The sign was worn. It was sad all of a sudden, picturing Johnny working here. She'd expected the store to somehow glow like he did, but what that might look like she didn't know. Edna couldn't contain her curiosity, and she dashed inside the place ahead of Grandma. It was a family grocery store. Behind the cash register was a blond girl who barely nodded when Edna said hello. Edna thought she might be just as vacant herself if she had to sit there all day behind the gum. This could be the "Jenny" who answered the phone when Grandma called in the ingredients for the Pineapple Upside-Down Cake. It didn't matter who she was, though; she was not fat or ugly, and therefore Edna was not happy she was there. She was a few years older than Edna and kind of pretty, but like many things here, she faded into the desert.

Edna floated down the narrow aisles, hoping to see Johnny at every turn. The idea that he might not be in the store grew heavy in her chest until she approached the very last corner. He was there. His back was to her. He wore a black T-shirt and Wranglers, and he was spraying water onto rows of vegetables. He was careful, going back over the peppers after he missed an area. Edna marveled at him and at her own power in being there. Her plan had worked. Johnny was right in front of her.

The bell on the door jingled, and Grandma yelled "Edna?" into the store. Johnny turned around.

"Hi, Edna. I didn't see you there."

"Hi," Edna said, and then her mind went blank.

"Are you looking for something?"

"Uh...shampoo."

"It's on the other side of the store, in aisle three."

He turned off the water and wrapped up the hose. Edna didn't know what to do, but lingering there for no reason was odd unless you had anything in the world to say. Grandma appeared.

"I need shampoo."

Edna left her and went directly to aisle three. The thing she hadn't planned was what she would do if she actually saw Johnny. Her face was hot, and blood rushed to her ears. She knew she was turning a blotchy crimson. She took a few deep breaths and summoned the mind control of a Tibetan monk. Observing things helped. She noticed how the old wooden floor was worn in the middle of the aisle. The store was clean, but it was crammed with so many products, it looked chaotic. She picked out the best bottle of shampoo they had and wondered how she could go back to Johnny without seeming as creepy as girls at school who said "hi" to boys too many times in the hall. She wasn't sure there was a way until she was able to convince herself that she had forgotten she wanted some broccoli. She hadn't had any broccoli in a while. She saw broccoli in the produce section.

Grandma waited for Edna near the girl who might be Jenny at the counter. The two women stood quietly. Some people, Edna reminded herself, don't always feel the need to engage. Instead of passing them, Edna searched the back of the store for the produce aisle, but the way she cut down didn't go through. The little store was a bit of a maze. She had no choice but to come around the front, passing Grandma and Jenny. They might notice she was prowling around for Johnny, but neither of them would say a word about it, even if it was obvious. Edna finally got to the produce aisle, but Johnny was gone. The hose he had been using was neatly coiled on a hook. Whatever kind of meaningful communication they could have had over a moment of grabbing some broccoli wasn't going to happen. Edna was crushed to have missed it. She tried to convince herself that maybe she was better off. Maybe Johnny hated broccoli. She wove around the aisles, looking for him for a little bit longer.

The door jingled again, and a man's enthusiastic voice rang out.

"Mary Miller? To what do we owe the extreme pleasure of this delightful visit?!"

"My granddaughter's getting shampoo."

Grandma didn't sound particularly moved by the effusive greeting. Edna was in a Johnny-seeking trance, but the store wasn't big enough to stay lost in for long. Defeated, she came to the counter with the shampoo. The old man who'd celebrated Grandma's presence rocked back on his heels and told Edna that she must be Edna. Edna nodded "yes." She had no words for the jolly man, but being Grandma's granddaughter, it didn't seem as odd as it might.

Grandma paid for the shampoo. They left the store. All Edna had gotten to say to Johnny was "shampoo." On the ride back, she realized she'd completely forgotten to ask about the oasis.

12
THE NEXT DELIVERY

Edna occupied herself by recreating the scene in the grocery store with a more preferred outcome during her long days filled with chores. She kept a little notepad that she found in the garage with her so she could jot down anything she wished she'd said. She was determined to make intriguing conversation the next time Johnny delivered groceries. So far the book was filled with sentences that were crossed out, except for the plan to ask Johnny if he knew about the oasis in the mural. She wondered if, in the past, asking people about things you could just Google instead was a way to connect with them. It might be a way to connect now. If Edna had Internet, she'd know exactly where the oasis was and lots of things about it, and she'd have nothing to ask. There were other things she'd Google if she could, like Johnny Bishop and dirt biking, but with no previous inclination toward dirt biking, she was likely to sound crazy trying to talk about it. It would not help make conversation. And it was creepy to mention things about a person you'd seen online. Everyone googled everyone, but it sounded like stalking if you admitted it. It was probably better that she knew nothing. Edna could only rely on what popped into her head.

The problem was, nothing did. Edna wanted to be nice and attractive, and she had no idea how to get a boy to like her, especially not within the few minutes of a grocery delivery once a week.

She moved her chair to face the ridge so she could see the truck coming. She'd be outside drinking coffee when he arrived. It was a mature, natural thing to do in the morning. Luckily, Grandpa wouldn't be out for some time yet to spoil the scene. She wasn't sure if Johnny would come at the same time he did last week, but it was as good a guess as any. The sunshine felt good. She wouldn't mind sitting there all day.

In the real world a million things would have happened in Edna's day before school. Edna had been ignorant of the dramas that had surely played out among her friends over the past weeks. She spent some time reading the 217 messages that came in when she turned on her phone in town. The first ones were mostly from Brit, and they evolved from anger (WT...??) to worry (R U OK??) to acceptance (spok 2 ur mom hv gr8 smmr). As Edna scrolled, the truncated words, presented all at once and out of context, became senseless. Edna had never been quite so out of the loop before, but she learned she wouldn't die from it. The loop would no longer compel her to check her phone every few minutes, every day, because she was afraid of dropping out of it.

Dust rose on the horizon, and then the little red truck came into view. It zipped across the basin. Edna reminded herself to stay calm. She hadn't thought of anything worth saying to Johnny in all the time she'd had, so instead she would marvel at the beautiful day and ask him if he had a nice ride out. In Shimmer, Jill wrote that men like women who are "happy and uncomplicated." Edna would try her best to seem happy and uncomplicated, even though she was exactly the opposite of that and hated following her mother's advice. It was the only advice she had.

Johnny pulled up and parked the truck by the porch, just like he did last time. He said, "Hi Edna" again as he went to the back of it. Suddenly Edna felt too far away from him as she sipped coffee in a chair. She shouldn't be immobile, distant, waiting for him to pass. It would only take one second for him to walk by her, and they would have no chance to talk. She'd have to jump out of her chair anyway. Why was she overplanning her every move? She abandoned her coffee drinking and followed Johnny to the back of the truck. He was taking Grandma's packages out.

"Isn't it a beautiful day?"

Her voice was too intense.

"Sure."

He took the groceries over to the house and Edna followed him.

"How was your ride out this morning?"

"Just fine."

"I love riding in the desert."

Edna hated how her voice sounded, but she persevered. She could talk to him now, or not at all.

"It must be like an adventure every time you deliver the groceries."

"I wish it were more of an adventure."

In the big room, Grandma said hello to Johnny, and he put down her packages.

"Wait, you have some extra stuff today."

Edna decided not to follow him back to the truck like a crazed puppy dog, but rather lingered on the porch like a young lioness ready to pounce. The fact that she didn't was an achievement in self-control. She ached to be close to him. It was a strange and inappropriate way to feel.

"You know, Mary didn't change her grocery order for a long time, until you came."

"Really?"

"She added jam a few weeks ago and then these things."

From the way Johnny shared this, Edna understood that she should be impressed. A jar of jam wasn't exactly an opulent welcome, but Grandma had, in fact, done something in advent of her arrival. Even the littlest thing was different from the nothing Edna thought she did, especially since she saw how little Grandma ever changed her routine.

Johnny put the groceries away with Grandma. Edna helped them. She noted that Johnny did not bring the canned goods into the pantry but left them on the counter this week. It was nice that he respected her privacy, but she hoped the vision of her underwear hanging from the shelves was receding from his memory. She also hoped she was going to think of something irresistible to say, and she wanted to be right next to him if she did. Feeling that she had to be happy and uncomplicated made it hard for Edna to think. She followed Johnny to the garage.

"Does Bishop's also fix cars?"

"No. I don't fix anything, just keep it running for Mary. Check the oil, take it for a spin every week."

"That's nice."

"Well, she pays me a little."

"It's still nice. I don't know what she'd do otherwise. Do you do that for a lot of people?"

"No, just Mary."

"Do you know anything about an oasis around here?"

"Sure, there's one at the inn."

"There's an inn?"

"It's, like, a bunch of cabins and a restaurant."

"With an oasis?"

"Yeah."

"I was curious about that mural in town, but I can't look anything up. There's no Internet here."

If Edna wasn't careful, she'd sound like she was complaining, one of the top ten ways to turn a man off, according to Shimmer.

In Johnny's experience, people didn't generally ask questions or talk much, especially to people they didn't know. It wasn't out of coldness, but more in the spirit of minding one's own business. Desert dwellers sought solitude and freedom, and minding their own business was what they did best. This girl from L.A. was probably bored out of her mind with her grandparents, who were the most extreme kind of solitude seekers.

"Do you feel like going for a ride?" he asked.

"Where are you going?"

"Just down the road and back."

Edna would have gone anywhere with him. If liking boys was a game, then hours of proofreading Shimmer for her mother finally gave her some advantage. She knew better than to seem too eager. With that in mind, she should say she was busy on such short notice, but under her circumstances, at her grandparents' cabin, that would have been impossible to believe.

When Johnny put on his Aviator sunglasses in the Bronco, Edna wondered if he knew he looked like a movie star. She couldn't see how he couldn't. If he lived in Brentwood, there would be no question he knew he looked like a star, and he'd probably act like one, too. A very bratty one.

"I don't want Mary calling the police again," he said as he pulled over by the cabin so Edna could jump out and tell Grandma where they were going. She'd never ridden in a car with a boy alone before. Her parents would not have allowed this at home.

Edna's time in the desert was mostly miserable, but it was occasionally more magical than anything in the real world. She'd had no idea she'd be going with Johnny to the oasis today. She was glad she hadn't known; she'd have been exhausted. She wouldn't have slept the night before.

13
OASIS

Edna gave up trying to think of the beguiling things she would say to Johnny if she were a happy and uncomplicated young woman. It was mentally straining, and it wasn't working. Everything she'd said was so dull it didn't come close to starting a conversation, and the sound of her own voice made her cringe. She was glad she had practice saying nothing with Grandma, because she really had to find a way to calm down.

They were only a few streets away from the stores in Desert Palms, in a neighborhood of charmless houses surrounded by colorless patches of dirt and delineated by chain-link fence. Edna was starting to doubt that an oasis as bucolic as the one in the mural could be near these scenes of neglect with abandoned cars on blocks and sagging laundry lines. But before they reached a dead end, there was a sign with an arrow that said: *Inn.*

Johnny turned into a long driveway lined with short, thick palm trees. Within a moment, the setting had transformed into the kind of shabby-chic luxury that could be found in a travel magazine. The driveway seemed to lead into the wilderness until a freestanding glass lobby came into view. Next to it was a rectangular swimming pool, lounge chairs and cafe tables, all elegant in their rustic simplicity. Beyond a grass lawn was a cluster of lush, tall palm trees surrounding a real pond. A soft chorus of birds was just loud enough to hear.

Edna was humbled; it was one of the most beautiful places she'd ever been to. When she had been lost in the desert, she'd thought it would be too much to expect a pretty little pond to die next to, but one existed after all. She would think twice about what was too much to expect in the future. As surprising as a pond in the middle of the desert was, a boat on the shady water was even more surprising. It was wooden with red trim, a quaint, gingerbread houseboat. On the water's edge, a deck had a rowboat tied to it. The scene was straight out of a fairy tale.

"Do they use that to get to the houseboat?"

He nodded.

"Let's check it out," he said.

He made his way over to the deck. Edna followed him.

"What if someone's in there?"

"Then the rowboat would be tied to it."

"What if the owner comes out?"

"I'll say, 'Hello, Aunt Betty.'"

"Oh."

Most kids Edna knew would have made a point of bragging that their family owned this hotel. Johnny held the boat as Edna got in it. The pond was small for actual boating, and a push was enough to coast to the houseboat. The damp air smelled like a mountain lake, and they were inside an invisible bubble of coolness. Johnny helped Edna up the steps on the side of the houseboat. Once aboard, they sat, their knees almost touching, on the houseboat's tiny patio in the improbable biosphere. Johnny wasn't only the cutest boy she'd ever seen, Edna thought, he was also really nice.

"Thanks for bringing me here."

"Sure."

"It's so beautiful."

"This isn't the same oasis as in the mural."

"There's another one?"

"Yeah, but the water's underground in that one now."

"Oh."

Edna looked up into the thick canopy of green. The palms swayed, and the sunlight sparkled around them. Insects swirled above the pond, catching light on their frantic journeys.

"Do you ever miss trees?"

"I never lived around that many," he said. "I just visit trees."

"I miss being around lots of trees sometimes."

"How long are you staying with your grandparents?"

"The whole summer, I think."

"They have trees."

"Just two."

"It's pretty far out, where they are."

"I guess so."

"You're nice to keep them company for so long."

"I try to be."

Edna wasn't about to tell Johnny that she was left with her grandparents because her parents were so frustrated they didn't know what to do with her. She also wasn't going to mention that she never once thought she was keeping anyone company. She couldn't tell Johnny much of anything about herself, but she didn't feel like that girl anymore anyway. If she changed into a new girl, the girl he thought she was, would it count? She stood up and noticed her reflection in the water. Would she have to tell him that she was kicked out of two schools? That he'd rescued her in the desert that day because she had been running away? Being in this beautiful place with this beautiful boy made Edna feel beautiful, too, but it still didn't help her think of anything to talk about. Shimmer advised asking something about the other person to start a conversation.

"How long have you been delivering Grandma's groceries?"

The question was stodgy on its own, and more so in the stunning surroundings.

"I've been driving for two summers, but we've been delivering your grandparents' groceries for, I think, seven years. I used to ride out there in the truck all the time. It's the furthest place we go."

"Did you ever hear my grandfather talk?"

"No, never did."

"He was in Vietnam."

Johnny nodded.

"There's lots of vets out here."

"I think he got sick after the war, not in it," Edna said. "I don't know what's wrong with him, really."

Johnny was trying to judge if Edna was a person he could talk to or not. The article in the paper said she was thirteen. Even if no one in her family had told her, he decided that she deserved to know about her own grandfather, and she looked able to handle what was pretty common knowledge about Ezekiel Miller.

"It's called obtunded, the thing he has."

"What's that?"

"It's like a…a reduced level of consciousness. They think it's from head injuries or PTSD."

Edna didn't know what that was either.

"Post-traumatic stress disorder."

"Oh. I've heard of that."

"And he was…he wasn't…doing that well around anything, uh, electrical, so they took over your dad's cabin. That was a long time ago."

He changed his mind; maybe it wasn't such a good idea to talk about this. He remembered when his dad had helped Mary chase Zeke down at the gas station. They'd finally changed the pumps to accept credit cards, and the beeping sounds they made flipped him right out. Johnny had watched as all three adults disappeared down the street, leaving him and little Pete alone in the backseat. He didn't share the story with Edna.

Even without it, this somewhat explained the weird setup of the cabin to her. She hadn't even known it belonged to her father. Edna felt uncivilized; Johnny knew more about her grandparents than she did. He'd shed some light on Grandpa, but Edna regretted bringing it up. It was a creepy topic, even if it was one of the few subjects she might have in common with Johnny. She would never bring her grandparents up with anyone at home. Edna never talked about them, and she didn't know until now that she was ashamed of them.

Two young couples came out of their cabins, a welcome interruption. One of the men tossed a volleyball into the air and yelled, "Hey, you guys wanna play?"

Four wasn't really enough for a volleyball game, considering his wife "sucked at it," he explained. One of the women, presumably the wife, punched his shoulder. Because of their trendy attire, Edna thought these artsy couples were probably from West Hollywood or Venice, and she proceeded to judge them. She was not an entirely new girl just yet. Bob, the guy who had called out to them, had an angry edge and was in his mid-twenties. He was soft, pudgy, and his fashionable eyewear did not make up for it. Bob's slight, fair-haired wife, Susan, was terrorized by him, and as a result she was a terrible volleyball player. Sherry, the female of the other couple, had dark skin, tattoos and blond dreadlocks. Edna didn't see how she could play volleyball with so many rings. Her boyfriend, William, wore jeans that were ripped by their designer.

It had been a while since Edna had played a game, and she'd do anything to stay out with Johnny. She said she'd love to. He didn't mind hanging out a little longer before spending the rest of the day cooped up in the store. He was getting a new bike at the end of the summer, but that didn't mean work was fun or easy.

The couples stayed as teams, and Edna and Johnny became the third person on each side. Edna couldn't wait to watch Johnny play, but a game never really got started. The other three only hit the ball to Susan, who leaned away from it in fear. The few shots she made flew wild and prompted a bizarre wrath from Bob.

"See what I mean? She's useless."

"Hey, play nice!"

Bob ignored Sherry and spiked the ball at Susan, cursing her mistakes.

"Ow!"

"Susan, that was a pass."

"Well, it hurt my hand!"

The ball rolled away. Bob and William laughed, too hard. Edna didn't know what was so funny, but they were strangely hysterical.

"Go get it," Bob ordered Susan, and he pointed toward the ball.

"You guys are mean," Susan yelled as she came back with it and whipped it at William.

Sherry supported Susan with, "Yeah, you guys really are."

Edna and Johnny were in the middle of some kind of psychodrama that had started before the volleyball game.

"We're gonna get going," Johnny announced.

"We're playing a game here. Don't be such a twit."

Johnny ignored Bob and his fake British accent. He looked to Edna and said, "Let's go."

"What's up, kid?"

"We have to get going. Thanks for the game."

"Really? Is there a problem?"

"No problem."

"All right, then!"

It didn't sound like it was all right, but Bob stuck his hand out to shake as Johnny passed. Johnny sighed and put his hand out in return, then Bob pulled his away. It was a lame joke, not worthy of acknowledging, and Johnny kept moving.

"Hey, kid. Kid!"

Johnny turned, only so this jerk would lower his voice.

"Why don't you just pop that cherry and get it over with?"

Edna tried to imagine what else that could have meant besides the crude thing it sounded like during the split second before Johnny hit Bob. Bob fell flat. It seemed like a pratfall, but then he didn't get up.

Johnny shook his hand out as he marched to the Bronco, pulling Edna, who, in shock, would have stood there indefinitely. They heard Susan as they left:

"That was awesome! I'm glad someone finally punched you in your fat face!"

Edna was too afraid to turn around. She didn't even notice that Johnny was holding her hand. Moments later they were driving through the sad neighborhood and into the open desert. The world fell into one of those quiets after something unbelievable has happened, but Edna couldn't let the incident fade away.

"Thanks for defending my honor."

"It wasn't that. I don't like being called a kid."

Edna smirked.

"You're not funny. That was a little dangerous."

"It was wrong."

He left out that he wasn't sorry, and he would do it again.

"Betty would be upset if she found out I hit a guest."

"Does your hand hurt?"

"No." He opened and closed his fingers. "Not too much."

"Do you get into a lot of fights?"

"No."

He was sincere. Edna loathed violence, but there was no denying she was pleased, and she found this disturbing. She wanted to curl up next to Johnny like a kitten now that he'd punched someone for her. It was sick. Instead of doing that, she looked at her watch.

"So those guys must be having a great vacation if they have to be drunk by ten in the morning."

"I don't know what they were on," he said under his breath.

"Are they going to be like that all day?"

"People come out here to do drugs."

"Do you do drugs?"

"No. Do you?"

"No! I don't know why you'd want to there. That oasis is even prettier than Hawaii. Maybe because it's so fragile. The bugs and frogs and everything would all die if they were only a few feet away from that spot."

"It's true."

"That must be why the town's called 'Desert Palms' and not just 'Desert.'"

He raised his eyebrow.

"I think so."

"I can't believe there are little fish in the pond. Did you ever sleep in that houseboat?"

"Sure."

"I'd like to stay there. It must be beautiful at night, especially with a full moon. Did you see how bright the moon was the other night?"

He nodded that he had.

"Yeah."

It might have been the idea of Edna in the moonlight, Bob's crude suggestion, or the combination of the two that made Johnny stop the Bronco. Edna was confused, she thought the Bronco had broken down, but Johnny didn't say a word. He slid close to her, assessed her face and softly kissed her. Soon his lips separated hers, and his tongue searched the inside of her mouth. She inhaled his breath. Edna had never kissed anyone this deeply before. She was terrified, and thrilled, and she had no idea what to do other than to let it happen. They clutched at each other with an urgency that came out of the blue. The muscles in his shoulders flexed, the ones he used when he was steering the dirt bike. He caressed her soft hair and the adorable curve at the small of her back. They were horizontal. Distant and then increasingly persistent alarms grew louder in his head. He could take Mary's granddaughter's virginity if he wasn't careful. On a dirt road, in their Bronco, no less. He had to tell himself a few times that this would *not* be a good thing. He made a low, involuntary sound as he peeled himself off this girl. He slid back behind the wheel and turned on the car. It sputtered before it started. He shook his head slightly.

"I shouldn't have done that. I just hit a guy for saying...I'm sorry. That was crazy."

He shifted the gears and drove on.

Edna's brain exploded, slowly, like a mushroom cloud.

Johnny liked her.

It was, at first, too foreign a notion to comprehend. As they rode on in silence, the only two people in an empty world, the blurry thought came into sharper focus.

"I can kiss, you know," she informed him.

"You should kiss someone your own age."

"Why?"

"It's safer."

"Why? You're not that much older than I am. I won't call you a kid if you don't like it, but you are still technically jailbait. The newspaper said you're seventeen."

She folded her arms and shrugged, as if he was no big deal.

"We're not going to do anything, Edna, and we shouldn't talk about it anymore either."

Most girls Johnny knew didn't challenge him. They wouldn't have had much to say about an oasis. They usually went on about some problem or how they felt fat, turning the topic, and his eyes, to their bodies. Before he knew it he'd be telling a girl that she wasn't fat and that he liked her body, and this usually led to some level of consummation, followed by crying later on when he got bored of it. Most girls Johnny knew had either been his girlfriend already or tried to be. It was a small town. In any case, it wasn't like him to ditch work, hit people and take advantage of thirteen-year-olds.

14
THE KISS

Later that day on the porch, Edna was feeling calm and very much like a woman. When she'd first heard that boys put their tongues in girls' mouths, she didn't believe it. She knew about sex, but somehow the part about tongues was even more disgusting. She was eleven. She thought she was being punk'd by these idiots at a party.

Edna knew everyone was kissing this summer, and if she hadn't been sent away, she would have been too, but it wouldn't have been anything like real kissing. Real kissing was way more fun than playing a game where you go into a closet and let boys do things to you. Edna was horrified when she found out that according to the rules of these games it could be any boy, even snot-nosed Jason Sinclair. Edna had watched him pick his nose all year. She refused to play and felt betrayed when Brit ended up in the closet with him. They'd always agreed: Jason was disgusting. In the last few years, Edna's society had become polluted with these games in which boys pressed their lips against girls' faces and flicked their tongues in and out. It was a waste of time, and she didn't see why she should kiss anyone she didn't even like. Feeling Johnny's tongue made her understand way more about sex than any of that, even more than the pornos she'd seen. No one even kissed in the pornos. Johnny's tongue made Edna understand a lot.

She was drunk from the kiss for the rest of the ride back to the cabin and scrambling for a way they could spend more time together.

"It's Grandpa's birthday coming up. We're going to make him a party on Saturday. You're invited," she threw off, as if she'd meant to mention it earlier. She congratulated herself for coming up with an idea and managing to get it out before he drove away for another week.

"This Saturday? I can't—"

"Not *this* Saturday. Next Saturday."

It wasn't a good idea to hang around Edna, but Johnny figured they wouldn't be alone at a party for Zeke.

"OK. I'll be there."

Edna would have made the party on any Saturday. She had no idea of the date, either of that day or of the next Saturday, or of her grandfather's birthday, but she would work it all out if Johnny was coming. She would legally change Grandpa's birthday if she had to.

The party idea must have escaped from the place where Edna stored annoying junk from Shimmer after the explosion in her brain. Nothing on Shimmer was real, the rules were all notions that Jill made up and passed off as if they were upper-class gospel. This particular notion was that if a woman liked a man, she shouldn't ask him out directly, but it was all right to host a party and invite him. Shimmer warned that you should be sure you liked the man a lot, since throwing a party required effort, especially, Edna thought, if you took all the advice on Shimmer about how to throw one. There were also probably some ideas about promising a birthday party at someone's house without asking them, especially if you didn't know when their birthday was, but Grandpa was unlikely to say he didn't want a party, or anything, to ruin it. So, a party was scheduled for next Saturday, but at the moment, Edna and Johnny were the only ones who knew about it.

Edna had a high standard of what a party should be. In the real world, birthday parties were a competition between parents and an art form for party planners who created installations worthy of museum exhibition for their four-year-old clients. Edna had no idea how to have a party here. In fact, it might not be possible; Grandma had made it clear that she never entertained. The cabin and the property around it were dismal. Edna had seen the town of Desert Palms, and she was certain there wasn't a party planner or an adequate party store in it. Lacking Google, she was beginning to feel like a part of her brain had been removed. She had to have some idea of how a party could happen before she approached Grandma and forced it on her, because Grandma was not likely to jump for joy. Edna remembered seeing some old phone books in the pantry.

The next morning she pulled out the phone books from where she'd hidden them under the couch. They were four years old. She'd never looked anything up in a phone book before. There were both yellow and white pages for the area designated "The Southern Desert Basin," and they were remarkably thin compared to other phone books Edna had seen, which she presumed was because there were no people here. Edna looked up the word "party." To her surprise, four party stores were listed. The first number she called was no longer in service, and neither was the next. At the third number someone answered in Spanish, and a baby cried in the background. Edna hung up. At the fourth number someone fumbled with the phone. It was an old woman.

"H-hello?"

She sounded like she used her phone about as much as Grandma did. Edna asked her if this was Party Central. The woman laughed.

"N-no dear, not for years."

"Oh, sorry to bother you."

"That's all right. God bless you, dear."

"Um, thank you," Edna said, and she added "you too," hoping that was a polite response to "God bless you" from a stranger on the phone.

There were no party stores in the vicinity. Or at least there weren't four years ago in the phone book, and Edna sincerely doubted that there were now. This party had seemed like a terrific idea when she came up with it in the Bronco, when she was thinking about things that might lead to more kissing and not at all about logistics.

Edna listed the only people she knew in the area. There was the jolly man she hadn't been friendly to at the store, the girl she thought was Jenny who didn't even turn around to say "hi," and the kind old lady she'd just called by accident. It was not a good list. The jolly man was all she remotely had going for her. Jolly Man certainly liked Grandma. Edna wondered if he might know of any nearby party planners until she realized, if he was milling around Bishop's, that he could be related to Johnny. Was Jolly Man Johnny's grandfather? Even if he wasn't, Johnny might find out that he was the first one invited to the party. It might be obvious that she had no party, that the whole party was being made after she'd already invited him and, by extension, because of their kiss. Sadly, as a source of information, Jolly Man was out.

If she were at Nanny's condo, Edna would ask around by the pool and everyone there would help her. In fact, the lipsticked old ladies would drop their bridge games to fight over who was doing what to make the party, and there would be too many people to invite within twenty minutes. Here there was no one to reach out to except Grandma. Or Grandpa. She might as well enlist a cactus. There was obviously no way to have this party.

Edna remembered how the pioneering Mrs. Anderson told herself to be strong as she looked at the impossible distance left to travel. She remembered that she herself was once hopelessly lost in the desert at nightfall with a dead coyote, and things still ended well. Edna had to be brave. It was too soon to give up.

"So, Grandma...?"

Grandma looked up from her dinner. Edna tried not to read too much into her hard expression. Maybe it was just how Grandma held her face.

"I was thinking about how we're going to make Pineapple Upside-Down Cake, and I guess Grandpa's going to have some, and I was thinking about Grandpa and how he doesn't usually see very many other people—"

Edna wasn't presenting this as well as she'd imagined.

"—I don't know...he must be in there somewhere, you know, because he can hear and see things and he definitely tastes food, and I thought it might be nice for him to have some people around while he was eating cake. I don't think he has that very often."

She felt like an idiot and couldn't stop rambling.

"And I don't remember ever celebrating his birthday with him *ever*, so I thought it could be like a birthday party if we want. Even if it wasn't really his birthday…"

She trailed off. Grandma's unchanging expression was too distracting, and a party, something Edna had in the real world once or twice a year, suddenly seemed like an outrageous ambition. And Edna had to create more urgency. Grandma might mull this over for a while. She had no way of knowing that Edna wanted an answer about having a party immediately, and to set the date too, for next Saturday. It might as well have been written in stone.

"So I was thinking about a week from—"

"I think that might be a bit much."

"What?"

"I said I think it might be a bit much."

Grandma looked down at her food. Edna had not heard the word "no," but she'd just hit a wall. Luckily, with the slow pace of Grandma's conversation style, Edna had an extended moment to react. She also had years of experience twisting things with her parents.

"What about it would be too much? It's just a little cake."

Grandma didn't answer.

"Grandma?"

"Edna, I said I think it might be a bit much—"

"But I'll do everything. And we're making the cake anyway. Do you mean too much for Grandpa?"

"Yes."

"Oh. Well, I know he's sick—"

Grandma's eyes widened but Edna continued.

"—but maybe he could use a little stimulation. Maybe we all could."

"Are you this disrespectful to your parents?"

"Oh my goodness, I'm much more disrespectful to my parents. What do you think I'm doing here?"

Mary looked hard at Edna. Her granddaughter might have a nice idea with the party, but she was too used to getting her own way. Edward was relying on her help with that, and Mary just couldn't get around Edna's disrespect. For Edna's part, she regretted her last comment. She always went too far for the drama of it or because she thought of something funny to say. But she was usually the only one who thought it was funny, and it did not move things forward. It never did.

"Grandma, I was just kidding about being disrespectful to my parents. And seeming proud of it. It was just a dumb joke."

"Apology accepted."

"So I was thinking that next Saturday—"

"Edna, I said I think a party might be a bit much."

Mary did not want to go on about it. She cleared her plate and went outside to get her husband. She thought it was funny that Edna could sit there for so long with that shocked look on her face. She didn't see how Edna could get anything out of Edward with it, so she figured it must appeal to some weakness in Jill.

There was only a glimmer of light left in the West. Mary still found the desert sunsets beautiful though she'd seen thousands of them. She moved the tray aside and took Zeke's hand.

"Let's go, honey bun. Time for bed."

Every evening she wondered: Would this be the time he finally wouldn't budge? But he balanced on his legs and made his way into the bedroom without her help.

Zeke hadn't said a word since "I love you, Mary," last winter. He'd gone a few months without a word before that. He used to talk in his sleep, but then that stopped, too. She could tell he was going to say something that last time because he grasped her hand extra hard as she pulled him up. He was conscious. Mary hoped he'd do that again, but she tried not to expect it so she wouldn't always be disappointed. Life was hard to believe these days, but she knew it wasn't permanent. The doctors said that when people with this kind of head trauma start to decline, they can go rapidly. She'd keep him comfortable for as long as he was breathing. She couldn't imagine living without her husband, though in the current state, she really wasn't living with anyone anymore.

It would never occur to Mary to make Zeke a party, but if Edna was going to do it, she wasn't sure she wanted to deprive him of it. It might be good for Zeke to be with people, more than it would be bad for Edna to get her way another time. He could still sense activity around him. Mary used to be sure she was doing exactly what Zeke would have wanted, but she was less and less certain of it all the time. It could be the last party he'd ever be at. Mary had to think about it.

15
IT'S ON

Edna had blown it with Grandma the night before, but like a hearty pioneer woman, she wasn't giving up so easily. She apologized profusely the next morning while continuing to make the case that the party was still a good idea for Grandpa, in spite of her terrible disrespect. Edna had a list of reasons memorized, but she didn't need them. In a surprising turn, Grandma agreed that they could have the party. Next Saturday was fine. Grandma's calendar was empty. Once again things that had seemed hopeless progressed.

"Is there anyone you'd like to invite?"

Mary furrowed her brow. A party might be more trouble than she thought.

"I'll think about it."

Later Edna found a list on the table. Grandma's writing said: *Sheriff Wegman and Mrs., Bill and Winnie Bishop, Johnny Bishop, Ken Bishop, Betty, Jenny, Shep Caulfield, Laura, Raul, Freddy.*

Grandma had surprised her: twelve guests was a healthy number. Edna never would have thought she knew that many people. Edna wasn't thrilled about inviting that sheriff who'd scolded her, but the more people at the party the better, with the exception of the kind-of-pretty Jenny. Edna briefly considered whether there was any way to not invite her. She was clearly on the list. Edna could be Machiavellian (she knew the word because her father accused her of being that way), but she decided she shouldn't do anything questionable. She would behave perfectly, at least as far as anything to do with Johnny was concerned.

Invitations were a huge consideration since they set the tone of any event, according to Shimmer, which of course recommended the best places to get them made. It was too late to get paper invitations for the party from any place good, and Edna doubted Desert Palms had a paper store anyway. Paper invitations were still the most effective, in spite of everyone's access to everything on their phone. It was statistically proven that people were more likely to come to your party if they received a paper invitation to it, and they dressed better, too. Shimmer had graphs illustrating the results of the studies.

From her grandparents' cabin, Edna had no way to send a cyber-invite either. Jill would be appalled. The last resort for inviting people to a party was by phone, because a phone call was never going to happen at a convenient time, according to Shimmer's Invitequette. ("Who wants to navigate a calendar while getting groceries into the car?") In fact, directly phoning people was almost considered an invasion of privacy, but Edna had no choice. She was inviting twelve people to a party, people she'd never spoken to before, all by phone. She usually liked doing things that would bother her mother, but this was not something she was looking forward to.

She wrote out a little speech. She noted that her prison sentence in the desert would be half over by the day of the party. The second half of Edna's summers always flew by as soon as she noticed their mid-point. She didn't mind being at Grandma and Grandpa's cabin anymore. Knowing she was insane didn't influence her feelings; Johnny had kissed her, and if nothing else happened, it was worth the entire summer. Somehow it was a defining moment, better than Maui and Paris and horseback riding and ice cream eating combined. One kiss beat all of that. Edna had always heard that people in love are crazy, and now she knew it for a fact.

There were so many things to consider before making her calls. The party had to start in the early evening because it was too hot outside during the day, and there was neither the space nor the air-conditioning inside the cabin for fifteen people to be comfortable. She wished she could invite everyone at night, when it would be even cooler, but there had to be some daylight. Grandma and Grandpa didn't have outdoor lighting. According to Shimmer, people can chat in darkness, but not for too long because it becomes a strain. Edna would light candles when it got dark, and the party would be ending soon anyway.

She practiced her speech and got up her nerve. Sheriff Wegman already hated her, so she called him first for practice. Edna could tell his voice mail was an old answering machine by the clicking sounds it made and the static beep at the end of his gruff recording.

"We're out, leave a message."

"Hello, Sheriff Wegman. This is Edna Miller, Mary Miller's granddaughter. I don't know if you remember me."

This felt horrible.

"We're having a celebration for my grandfather, Zeke Miller, on Saturday, July 31 at six p.m. at 71200 Cottontail Trail in Dream Valley, and you and Mrs. Wegman are cordially invited. Grandma is making her award-winning Pineapple Upside-Down Cake. We hope you can make it."

Edna fell short of saying that it was actually Grandpa's birthday. She still didn't know when it was. She kept forgetting to ask. She didn't really want to know because it probably wasn't soon, and she didn't need any more reasons to feel stupid while making these phone calls.

"Bishop's," a voice answered. It was Jolly Man, who was probably Johnny's grandfather.

"Hello, I'm calling for Bill or Ken Bishop?"

"This is Bill."

Edna tried not to sound like she was reading off a page when she invited him to the party, but she still felt the strain in her voice.

"Well, we'd be delighted, Edna."

"Great. Is Johnny there?"

"No, he's not. Shall I give him the same message?"

"He already knows about it, but I hadn't told him the time yet."

"I certainly will tell him."

She was being so mature, not needing to track him down. Pretending to be a happy, uncomplicated girl could be fun sometimes.

"Is Jenny there?"

"Why, yes."

He handed over the phone.

"Hello?"

"Is this Jenny?"

"Yeah."

It was the hardest invite yet.

"This is Edna Miller. I'm Mary Miller's granddaughter."

There was silence on the other end. A person might say "hi" or "I saw you at the store" or something. Edna leaned against the wall, twirling the phone's long cord.

"We're having a party for my grandfather next Saturday at six, and you're invited."

"Seriously?"

"Yes."

"Um, OK. Yeah, I guess I can go."

"Terrific. See you then."

16
THE LOGISTICS

The phone rang off the hook for a few hours compared to its normal silence. Everyone who had been invited to Grandpa's party had either answered the phone or RSVP'd right away, and they were all coming to the party. Edna found this unusual. She was used to her world, where degrees of busy-ness denoted standing. No one would immediately RSVP. At Jill's seminars women often greeted each other with:

"How are you?!"

"Oh, busy. Crazed. Absolutely crazed."

"Oh, me too. I'm *totally* crazed."

Edna pictured these crazed women flailing around the shops, cafés and freeways of Los Angeles.

The initial steps that had seemed insurmountable—solidifying the date for the party and inviting people—were conquered, but there was no time to enjoy these victories. Edna had no idea what in the world to do with these people for several hours; eating a piece of Pineapple Upside-Down Cake would only take a few minutes. Parties had DJs or activities like attending a concert or a Lakers' game, rock climbing or snorkeling. There was nothing to do here. And as quick as it may be to have a piece of cake, there wasn't even anywhere to eat it. Edna looked around her grandparent's bleak compound. Their two-seater picnic table might squeeze four. The dead weeds around it shook in the wind and seemed to taunt her, saying, "Go ahead. Try to make this place festive."

Inside, the kitchen table barely fit her family around it when they were having a soda, never mind fifteen people with forks and plates. In any case, the table was strangely bolted to the floor and not in a convenient spot for people to walk around. There definitely weren't enough chairs. Edna had invited a dozen people over, and she couldn't even offer them a place to sit down.

In the real world, parties were assigned a planner, a theme and booked. Perfect Party did her last birthday, and Edna wondered if they would come to Dream Valley. Why couldn't she order a party over the phone with her emergency credit card? If this was not an emergency, Edna didn't know what was. She simply had to have a great party.

She knew she'd get in trouble for spending money without asking, but her parents would have already have seen pictures of the party by the time they got the bill. They might think it was a good thing for her to have done. It was something they'd do themselves, if they'd thought of it. Edna was sure she was doing the right thing, and even if not, they wouldn't be as mad as if she bought games or a new iPad.

They still had "information" on landlines. Grandma had written down the number by the phone, so Edna was able to call Perfect Party once Grandma was outside and absorbed in moving rocks around her garden. The woman who answered was named Janice, and she sounded really nice. Edna did her best to sound like an adult. She loved ordering things; it was like waving a magic wand. Perfect Party had tables, chairs, glassware and catering. Edna ordered whatever she wanted or thought she might want in both white and blue. She needed a masculine color for Grandpa, but without pictures she couldn't decide, so she'd choose once she saw them. Or maybe she would mix them. Perfect Party could set up anywhere they could drive to in less than five hours, and Dream Valley was only four hours away. All Janice needed was Edna's credit card, and Edna felt very grown up saying the numbers to her. Janice had to run the card. Edna waited for a long time before she came back to the phone.

"Edna, honey, I'm afraid you're beyond the limit on this card for the deposit."

Edna had no idea that her credit card had a limit, but when she called the number on the back of it, she found out it was five thousand dollars. Whether that was a lot or a little for a deposit on a party didn't matter as much as the fact that she couldn't get a party brought out to Dream Valley with it. It wasn't even enough when she cut what she asked for in half, and only in one color. If five thousand dollars wasn't enough for a party deposit, it was not sufficient emergency funding for anything, and she planned to discuss this with her parents sometime when she was speaking to them again. Edna's only source of money was those tyrants, but she couldn't beg them to pay for this. With an over-five-thousand-dollar deposit, it was expensive enough for Jill to butt her nose into so she could control everything and, God forbid, be at. There was no point in having the party if there was any chance of that. Even Nanny wouldn't help. Edna had asked her for money once, and Nanny had told her parents. She was crushed by the betrayal, and her allowance had been cut off for two weeks.

Edna couldn't come up with an idea of how to have the party, but the day she invited everyone was going to come whether she liked it or not.

If the midday sun had a sound, it would be one of those menacing vibrations that drove people insane. This wasn't helping. She got that scary, claustrophobic feeling, and her chest was tight. She was trapped at the cabin with nothing but her grandparents' ugly furniture. She didn't even see how Mrs. Anderson, with all her strength and tenacity, could find a solution to this problem. Could Mrs. Anderson chop down the eucalyptus trees and build a table and fifteen chairs with them?

Sick of looking at the porch and the cabin, Edna went down to the garage. She had been spending more and more time there. It should have had room for two cars, but it was crammed with stuff and barely fit the Bronco. It had cracks that let in wind and sand. Furniture that had come here from San Diego had never been unwrapped, but it was getting beaten down by the desert anyway, even under the blankets protecting it. The cabin didn't have much room for furniture, but it wasn't like it was ever going to. What was Grandma saving it for? Edna turned around the taxidermied raccoon and fox that stared at her. She couldn't move the giant fish, so she just had to deal with its giant eyeball. She was eventually able to ignore it. Her grandparents must have been outdoorsy; their old tent leaned against a wall. It was more than likely unusable; Edna's tent let in rain after being stored for two years. They'd probably never go camping again anyway.

It was weird to get to know someone after the fact when they weren't dead yet, but being in Grandpa's garage was a way for Edna to retroactively get to know him. He had been some kind of nutty tool collector, he had a mountain of rusty implements. Edna wasn't sure how long it had been since Grandpa did things. Grandma seemed pretty organized, so the mess was probably his after years of neglect. Maybe it was left like this because of his illness. Edna wasn't handy, but she put the different rusty items that looked alike together and created a tidy workshop a little at a time. She wondered if Grandpa would appreciate this, or if he was the type of person who clung to his chaos.

A sheet-metal case dominated a part of his worktable. She opened the bottom drawer first. It was mayhem, packed with crusty batteries, flashlights, wire, more rusty tools, nuts and bolts, markers and pencils. She couldn't even open it without emptying some out. Edna normally hated any kind of disorganized clutter, but this could be information. The air hung still and sweat dripped down her nose. Edna was so interested in Grandpa's things, she didn't even notice.

The second drawer was filled with cassette tapes. They were deteriorated; Edna couldn't play them even if she had the machine to play them on. She decided to put Grandpa's music on her phone when she got home. She found a faded notepad from the Sand Castle Inn of Pismo Beach and wrote down what Grandpa's music was. Edna had heard of Elvis Presley, the Beach Boys and the Rolling Stones, but she'd never heard of Jan and Dean, Hank Williams, the Kinks or the Ventures.

There were nails sticking out of the wall behind the table, and Edna hung tools on them as she thought about the logistics of her doomed party. Grandma was making Pineapple Upside-Down Cake for fifteen people, and it had to be fantastic. She couldn't do that and be much help with anything else while she still had to take care of Grandpa. Anyway, Edna had promised to do "everything." She had no idea how, and she couldn't imagine what could change between today and then. It would have been easier to cancel the party when Johnny was the only one coming. This problem was not going away like it was supposed to.

She heard a faint, chirping sound coming from the loft, but she didn't see the bird making it. The garage was so cluttered, she'd never looked up and noticed all the stuff stored above. Three surfboards rested on the rafters, each with a colorful design that had dulled over the years. They didn't seem to belong in the desert, but they probably went fine with San Diego and Pismo Beach. Beneath the surfboards, bundles were tied off to the beams in a messy web of straps and bungees. The web held two metal folding tables.

17
THE BREEZY PERSONALITY & THE DIRT

Johnny had gotten a haircut. Edna was shocked, though she knew boys often cut their hair short in the summer. She wasn't sure if he was cuter with his hair long and wild or cropped short because he looked so good both ways. She might like it better long, but she liked it even better that he wasn't attached to his hairstyle. She liked seeing more of his face. She liked seeing him.

"Hey, Edna."

"Hi. How was your ride out?"

"Just fine."

He always said it was just fine. It was a boring question, but she was still trying to sound easygoing and not too challenging. The breezy personality was working well. Johnny'd kissed her with the breezy personality. The breezy personality reminded her to act like a viable young woman and not an anxious, silly girl. Johnny went to get Grandma's packages from the back of the truck.

"Nice haircut."

"Thanks."

"Johnny…"

"Yeah?"

"Would you help me get something down from the garage, for the party?"

"Sure. Be right out."

He brought Grandma's packages inside. Moments later Edna and Johnny walked down to the garage. Holding his hand would have been natural. It was only inches away from hers.

Johnny raised his eyebrow when he looked at the complicated bundles strapped to the beams. Edna loved to see his eyebrow go up when he was thinking, but this time she knew it was because the favor was more than he'd bargained for. She'd become a nuisance. She hadn't considered the ton of random junk stashed up there in the way of the tables. She had been so excited about the tables to begin with, and then that she could ask Johnny to help her and have an excuse to interact with him. He got a big ladder and had to unhook a horse's saddle and some fishing poles. He carefully handed them down to Edna. He looked around the rafters.

"Holy sh—there's a bunch of guns up here."

He took out a rifle from a long case that was dried out and falling apart. It was tied next to the surfboards. Johnny evaluated the rifle and saw that it wasn't loaded. Clearly Johnny had handled guns before. Edna wasn't sure, but this might have been the first time she'd ever seen a real gun and not a picture of one, or one that was a toy. No, she'd seen handguns on police, but not rifles or shotguns like these. Guns, in Edna's realm, were part of what was wrong with the world, and no one should have them. Grandpa had a few different kinds. Johnny's comfort with them mystified her. He checked them one at a time and set them on the area of the counter Edna had recently cleaned off.

"What do you think they're doing here?"

"I don't know. Zeke probably shot a little bit."

"Oh."

"Everybody has guns."

"They do?"

"Uh-huh. Do you shoot?"

"No. Never."

"It's fun."

"Really?"

Edna couldn't imagine why it would be fun. Moments later Johnny set some cans from Grandma's recycling out on rocks.

"That's about fifty feet, a pretty good distance for a BB gun."

He put some BBs into the gun, pumped it and handed it to Edna, who immediately recoiled from it.

"Tsk. No way."

"Take it."

"I don't know how."

"Go ahead and aim."

Edna took it. She found one of the cans in its sight.

"That's pretty good. You even have the butt tucked into your shoulder."

"I've seen people aim rifles on TV."

He moved her elbow down.

"Take a shot."

She took one and looked after it. She'd missed, but she couldn't tell by how much.

"These aren't the right BBs for this gun, so it might be spinning off a little high and right."

He looked into the sight and re-aimed the gun.

"Try to compensate a little low and left."

Edna tried to compensate for the spin and for being thrown off with Johnny so close to her. She pulled the trigger. The can flew off the rock. She'd shot something, and she was actually proud of it.

"I did it!"

"Try it again."

She missed the next two shots in a row.

"Pull the trigger after you exhale."

"Seriously?"

He shrugged. "Yeah."

Edna took aim.

"Don't forget to compensate."

She looked down the sight and estimated what she thought Johnny would have compensated. She inhaled, exhaled, and in a moment of stillness she pulled the trigger. The can flew off the rock.

"You're a good teacher."

"No, you're a natural."

"You go."

"Finish 'em off."

"No, you go.

She had to see him shoot. He aimed the gun and shot the first one clean. He missed the next one but tried again and hit it. He got all the cans that were left from where he stood. He thought it was funny that Edna was so impressed.

"It isn't hard. You just did it."

"Hey!"

She gave him an affectionate push. A quick memory of being on top of her in the Bronco flashed through his mind.

"Come on," he said, "let's get the tables."

The mundane chore was a thrill for Edna. Johnny got on the ladder and reached up to undo the worn, leather straps holding them, which were actually old belts buckled together and knotted around the beams. The belts were so dried out, it was probably good they were taking this stuff down. Edna wondered if Grandpa did all this or if Grandma could have done it, or if her father or some other crazy person had. It was hard to imagine someone fastening these belt buckles together or understand why they didn't just use rope. She tried to picture her grandparents storing their things or walking into the garage for the first time, but she abandoned that pursuit when she noticed Johnny's T-shirt hiking up as he fought with the belt buckles. She could see his stomach.

Edna had seen boys in bathing suits year-round all her life, but she had never taken particular note of any boy's stomach before. It was flat and had a faint line of hair beneath his navel. He reached higher, exposing more of it.

"Watch out, there's a lot of—"

A dove flew out of the beams, startling Johnny, and he dumped years' worth of old birds' nests and debris that was trapped behind the tables onto Edna. Twigs, dirt and feathers fell onto her face. She felt a hundred little pricks in her eyes, and she gasped as she was momentarily blinded, breathing in dirt. A nest filled with chicks landed next to her, and their piercing squeals terrified her more.

"Edna. Oh my…let's get you to the house."

Johnny got down the ladder just in time to keep her from stepping on the nest. He picked Edna up and put her into the Bronco. She didn't take her hands away from her face while he drove up the slope.

"What was that noise?"

"There were some chicks. Are you OK?"

"I think so. Did the chicks die?"

"No. Edna, I'm sorry—"

"It was an accident."

She went straight into the bathroom. Edna cried intensely. She had reasons to be upset, but none of them seemed to justify such deep emotion. The dirt came off easily. She couldn't stand to think about what she must have looked like with that dirt all over her. It was a slap in the face from fate, really, when she tried so hard to look good around Johnny. The worst thing was that he'd picked her up and she didn't even enjoy it. Still, none of these things matched her distress. She didn't come out of the shower for a long time. Grandma knocked on the door.

"Are you all right, Edna?"

"Yes."

Crying over boys was exactly what Edna had been avoiding for the entire last year. She missed her old self, who couldn't care less about a boy. Her old self might have gone as far as to think Johnny was an idiot for dumping dirt on her, but now she would never think that. If she hadn't met him in the first place, she'd have easily convinced her parents to end this stupid punishment and she would have been out of there weeks ago, but she would never think of that now either. Edna didn't know what to think. She came outside in her bathrobe. The heat felt good after crying for so long in the shower. It was good to dry out.

The red truck was gone. Johnny had brought the tables up to the porch. He'd opened them and hosed them down. At least Edna assumed he had, because it probably wasn't Grandma. Together the sturdy, metal folding tables would be long enough for everyone at the party to sit at. A note on one of them was held down with a rock, written on a blank Bishop's receipt:

Edna, Really sorry again. Let me know if you need anything else for the party. J

His handwriting was blockish and looked like a boy's, but it wasn't sloppy. It was perfect, like everything else about him.

18
SOUVENIRS

"Grandma, do you have any idea where we can get fifteen chairs?"

"Well, I think I have four or five chairs. Some people could sit on the couch inside or on the porch steps."

This marked the end of Edna's interest in Grandma's opinion of anything to do with the party.

While Bishop's was called a general store, it was really more of a supermarket. It probably did not sell folding chairs like other variety stores might. Still, the Bishops were the only people Edna knew who might help her with chairs. It would be the final favor she'd ask of Johnny. He said she should let him know if she needed anything else; in fact, he'd put it in writing. She definitely needed chairs. She had to order groceries for the party anyway. She dialed the store.

"Bishop's."

It was him.

"Hi, Johnny. It's Edna."

"Hi."

She thought this was a more special "hi" than he might give anyone else, that he sounded happy to hear from her.

"Thanks for bringing the tables up last week. And for cleaning them. And for getting them down."

"Sure. Sorry again about...what happened."

"It's OK. The chicks were gone when I came back."

"I put the nest back up there."

"Oh."

She liked picturing him doing that. Edna was sure a coyote had eaten them. There was a lot of proximity to death in the desert, but not this time. She went over her party list. Johnny was cute with the attentive way he said "uh-huh" to everything and wrote it all down, even if this was normal behavior for someone taking an order over the phone.

"And can you think of anyone with chairs that I could borrow? Or where I could buy some?"

"I could borrow some from Betty. How many do you need?"

"Fifteen. Please."

"Big party, Edna."

Edna was well on her way to becoming a new girl: she was excited about getting tables and chairs for her party and did not take them for granted. Still, tables and chairs were not nearly enough to transform the place. The next mission was to decorate.

"Grandma, do you mind if I use stuff from the garage for the party?"

"No."

"I can use whatever I want?"

"If it's in there, Edna, you can use it."

Edna abandoned the rusty tool section she had been working on and rooted through the garage like the mouse in Grandma's pantry.

She thought a box of Christmas decorations would be a jackpot of possibilities, but Grandma's ornaments were sad and covered in a film of oldness, like all of her things. The yellowing balls were painted with somber images of Jesus in the manger or on the cross. Edna's family had much cheerier ornaments for Christmas. The only things she liked were Grandma's white lights. They had big bulbs, which Edna preferred. If she could string them from the cabin to the eucalyptus trees, they would look nice lit up at dusk. Edna went outside to see if she thought she could. She needed the big ladder. It was heavy, and she probably couldn't carry it to the cabin all the way from the garage.

Mary was shocked when she saw what Edna had been up to in there. She hadn't realized the garage was so chaotic until some of it was cleaned up. She never went into that garage. Mary feared her delicate state of mind wouldn't sustain a challenge from all her old things. Instead, she was inspired by her granddaughter's drive. Together, they were strong enough to get the ladder into the back of the Bronco. It hung out the back, but that was all right. It was fun sitting on the rungs, weighing it down so it wouldn't fall out while Grandma drove it up to the cabin. The ladder was twelve steps high, and Edna needed help every time she had to move it. Eventually, Grandma told her to finish hanging the lights later when the sun was lower. It was just too hot to drag around a heavy ladder.

Grandpa had a collection of old, embroidered handkerchiefs, and Edna thought it would be fun to use them as napkins. This meant bleaching and, of course, ironing them, which was another thing she could only do after dinner because of the heat. She started napping in the middle of the day and working into the evening so she could get more done. Soon Edna's whole life revolved around making the party.

She crafted flowers out of wire and tissue paper and arranged them in Grandpa's old bottles. She put together a set of silverware from what she could find in odd drawers in the pantry. Real silver was nicer than Grandma's boring, old-person stainless, which there wasn't enough of anyway. The silver was tarnished, but Edna remembered how to clean it using water, baking soda and tin foil from an article in Shimmer. She hated to admit that she was glad to have some of these tips. During this break from her mother, Edna could see that there were a few good things about her. Shimmer might actually be helping people.

Sand had made its way into a box of wine glasses in the garage, through the folds of the paper protecting them. Edna found it hard to imagine Grandma throwing a dinner party and putting out the pretty crystal stemware cut with a delicate star pattern. She must have been a different woman when she got all these things. Nothing she did now made it seem like she missed them, but there was still something sad about the fact that Grandma never needed anything nice. Edna found a crumpled picture in the box with the glasses. It was of Grandma and Grandpa, taken around the same time Grandma won the prize at the San Diego County Fair. It was a humble wedding photo, and Edna hoped it was one of many because it was worn out and creased. She wondered why'd she'd never seen this before, but she remembered how Grandma reacted when she saw herself in the old newspaper article. She decided not to ask about it. It was strange that she felt proud of Grandpa in his Marine uniform, because what she'd learned about wars and fighting them was that they were always bad. He looked handsome, strong and completely conscious. She liked his smile. Grandma smiled here, too. She wore a pretty white dress and held flowers and had everything to live for. They were a gorgeous couple by a beach. Maybe it was Pismo Beach, from Grandpa's notepad. She kept the pad, in case it was, with the photo, and saved them with Johnny's note on the Bishop's receipt and the article in *The Desert Weekly*. She was accumulating quite a few souvenirs.

Making this party required the effort of a young pioneer woman preparing for a cross-country trek. Luckily, Edna had practice with the chores she'd been doing for weeks and a lifetime of arts and crafts projects. Having goals made the time pass, and being with Johnny for a few hours would be more than worth it, though Edna confessed to herself that she didn't entirely understand why. In any case, the week flew by with so many tasks, and it seemed like no time at all before the red truck zipped through the basin again.

Edna sipped her coffee and watched it through the window in the big room this week. She shouldn't be waiting outside for Johnny every time he came over. Shimmer said it was good to create mystery with a man and not linger, always available. Edna didn't know if love meant presenting herself as the opposite of who she was, but it was working. As far as Johnny was concerned, she had things to do; she didn't even remember he was coming this morning. He parked and looked over for her before he went to the back of the truck. Good. Edna waited. She waited longer. Was he kidding around with her? What was taking so long?

When she was too curious to be mysterious any longer, she went out to the back of the truck. Johnny had a cooler and ice, and he was putting in perishables.

"Oh. I didn't think of that."

"Hey. I figured you needed someplace to put all this."

He put in more ice on top.

"Johnny, do most people you deliver to have iceboxes or refrigerators?"

He laughed.

"Most people have refrigerators."

"What's so funny?"

"Do you think people here have no television or refrigerators? We know about Google, you know."

"Well, Grandma and Grandpa don't know about it."

"No, they sure don't. What do you do out here all day, anyway?"

"I paint the porch. I read after dinner."

"Doesn't sound too bad."

Edna couldn't get used to the roller-coaster-like rushes that came whenever she was with him. She'd heard of this. It could have been because of the way he smiled or the way he made her feel better about her pathetic summer, but analyzing it was only accentuating it. She saw the fifteen wooden folding chairs he'd brought, all white, packed in the back of the truck.

"Those are the only kind she has."

"They're perfect."

Other boys had liked Edna in the past. Jason Sinclair texted her fifty-six times in one day, and Brian Sutcliff cried over her in front of everyone in the gym. Neither of them was smart enough to be this nice.

19

THE DAY OF

When the desert sand was clean, it looked more exotic. Edna liked it better than the scrub-covered desert she was in. She pulled every weed growing near the cabin out of the ground. It gave the space definition, and it became its own sort of oasis from the wild. She had a new appreciation for what it took to keep the desert elements tamed, and she finally understood why Cleopatra was always bathing and primping herself in the old, biblical movies that came on TV around Easter. It took an entire army just to keep the sand out of her tent and off her plush pillows and rugs.

Edna overlapped Grandma's old Oriental rugs on the ground under the tables to make the space look more like a dining room. She knew it would be impossible to get all the sand off them afterwards, but the guilt she felt about it did not override how much better it looked. They were rolled up in the garage and would probably never be used again anyway. Grandma's tablecloths were a nest for mice and completely ruined, so Edna used white sheets instead. With the rugs underneath and Grandma's good dishes finally out, the table reminded her of a scene in one of her father's films, an officers' dinner during the British occupation of someplace in North Africa. Or it resembled the scene from a distance. There were too many improvisations, like the sheets, the homemade flowers and the mismatched silverware. Still, it was charming, maybe because it was unique and not so serious. In any case, Edna decided it was better than what she'd have paid thousands for if she'd hired Perfect Party.

Grandma started baking before sunrise, whipping batter, lining the bottoms of cake pans with pineapple rings and putting chopped cherries and walnuts into their holes. While things were heating or cooling, she dressed herself and Grandpa. Whether Edna realized it or not, this was a special occasion for him and a ton of work for her. It hadn't occurred to Edna that Grandma might have needed help making three Pineapple Upside-Down Cakes, but if she did, she was out of luck. Edna had to rearrange furniture, clean the whole cabin and make herself beautiful before six.

Edna took extra care with her hair and her makeup, and she experimented for the first time with putting tissue in her bra. She knew other girls did this. She thought it was idiotic to attract a boy to something he might eventually find out was fake, but she hoped she was not fully developed yet, so she could eventually make good on a false impression. She wished she was just a little older. She was careful not to put in too much tissue. She'd just seen Johnny three days ago, and it was a fine line between an artful enhancement and a freakish growth spurt.

Thirty minutes before the party, Grandma and Grandpa sat on the porch, completely ready. Grandpa was shaved and had a haircut. He wore a white button-down shirt with a navy sport jacket and matched the party well enough, even if there was no cure for the vacant expression on his face. Grandma looked exactly like she did when they went to town.

"You and Grandpa look really nice."

Edna meant it, but she was also hoping to raise Grandma's spirits a touch, which might make her a better co-hostess. It was hard to imagine that twelve people would be coming shortly and that Grandma would have to greet them all. Edna wondered if Grandma would say anything about her chest, but she only said, "You look nice too, Edna."

Edna sat on the ugly couch inside for a while before she went back to the bathroom and took the stuffing out of her bra. She couldn't forget it was there. She was nervous enough; there was no point in being more self-conscious. When she came out onto the porch, the wind had disappeared. The world was quiet. Dust rose over the hill, announcing the first guests' arrival.

20
THE PARTY

Motorcycles cut up the dirt road, and the leather-vested riders howled louder than their engines.

"Zeke! Zeke, you nut!"

They came so close to the cabin, Edna thought they were going to drive right up the porch. They dumped their bikes and charged over to Grandpa without even acknowledging that Edna and Grandma were there. Edna had an immediate aversion to the men. They shook Grandpa's chair.

"Look at 'im!"

"All gussied up in a suit!"

It's not a suit, it's a jacket, Edna thought, *but whatever.*

The one named Freddy handed Grandma a six-pack of sodas. Edna would try to remember that Raul had the longer, gray ponytail, and that Freddy was fatter, which started with "F." Raul and Freddy were a little younger than Grandpa. Their vests were covered in patches, and their skin had tattoos about MIAs and POWs. Edna knew it had something to do with Vietnam, something bad. She'd add it to her list of things to look up when she got home. The list was getting pretty long.

"You must be Edna."

"Yes. Thanks for coming today."

"It's real nice of you to throw this party for your grandpa."

"Thank you."

Raul added, "And he has a nice granddaughter."

"Oh. Thank you."

It didn't exactly make sense, but Edna wasn't really listening. She was reading one of Raul's tattoos. It was a dog tag with the inscription:

I will be strong and courageous.
I will not be terrified or discouraged.
The Lord is with me wherever I go.

She thought it was heavy that he kept these words in a place where everyone could see that he needed them. It made her uncomfortable. She watched for more cars coming across the ridge and reminded herself to relax. Of course everyone was coming. It was only thirty seconds into the party.

The men cracked open soda cans and sat at Grandpa's feet on the porch. This wouldn't have been the scene Edna had in mind for the rest of the guests to walk into: two round-bellied bikers guzzling on the steps, hollering at their man Zeke. People might think Edna had given them their cans of no-name cola, which she would never serve, but if she did, she wouldn't serve it in a can. She didn't ask anyone to bring anything in the first place. She was careful to sound sweet when she said, "Would you guys like to sit in chairs?"

"No, this is fine."

Freddy stretched his feet down to the next step.

"That's a beautiful table, though."

"Yeah, it's beautiful," Raul agreed.

"Way too nice for here."

"Thank you. Excuse me."

Edna's heart pounded at the sight of the red delivery truck, and she ran in its direction to get a better view. She liked seeing it at a different time of day, and with the sun at another angle she could read "Bishop's General" from much further off, although she couldn't see inside. Soon she realized she shouldn't be standing there intently focused on the truck's progress toward the cabin in front of Grandma and the bikers, and Johnny, for that matter. She went inside and counted to ten. She had to remind herself to be easy and breezy and not to run up to Johnny like a refugee at a food drop. When she came out again, the truck was parked, and the driver's side door opened. A leg in sports pants stuck out and jostled around before the person attached to it emerged. For a moment Edna wondered if it was at all possible that Johnny ever wore synthetic, beige sports pants, but Johnny's grandfather, Bill, stepped out of the truck. His wife, Winnie, got out of the passenger side.

"Mary Miller! Mary, do you know the last time I was out here was years ago? I don't even know how many," Bill shouted.

"I have no idea," Grandma responded flatly.

"It must be Edna! I've seen you twice since she's been here. You have a magical granddaughter. A very magical granddaughter!"

His enthusiasm was slightly ridiculous, but Edna was a little charmed.

"Hi, Mr. Bishop."

"Hello, young lady. Look, Winnie. Look at this table!"

Winnie wore a white top with a blue flower print and matching blue pants. She squealed when she saw the table. She was a female version of her husband.

The rest of the guests arrived, except for the most important one. Edna thanked Johnny's Aunt Betty for her chairs and realized she must have been his great-aunt. A frail woman named Laura was introduced to Edna as Grandpa's home-care therapist from years ago.

"I tried for to bring Zeke out of his shell, and he'd come out of it now and then for a long time, but that last time he fell into it, I think that might have been for good."

Laura lived in a place called Thompson Valley that she described as "really remote." In this context Edna had no idea what that could mean. Thankfully, Laura was enticed by how much bigger Grandma's garden was than the last time she had been there, and she had to go take a look. Small talk was challenging, even though most of it was complimenting Edna on how pretty she was and how nice it was of her to make a party for her grandparents. All Edna could see was that, so far, every one of these guests had gray hair. It was depressing. Her party looked like an old-age home. She had known most of the guests would be older adults, but Edna hadn't considered this possibility. No one had gray hair in Brentwood, not even old people.

Shep Caulfield asked Edna where the bathroom was, and she went inside to show him. He hadn't even bothered to brush his gray hair. When she came out again, an old, blue Jeep was parking with the rest of the cars. Jenny from the store got out of it, slammed the door and walked toward the cabin. She seemed angry and aloof and, to Edna, way too beautiful. She didn't remember the girl she saw in the store as that pretty, and she would have thought twice about accidentally not inviting Jenny if she did. Her backlit blond locks bounced around her shoulders. Johnny got out of the driver's side, which could only mean that he'd driven the Jeep while she was in it. He took off his sunglasses. He said something to Jenny that Edna couldn't hear, and Jenny shrugged and ignored him. Johnny shook his head.

Edna tried to think of how what she was looking at could be anything other than a fight between a boyfriend and a girlfriend, but she couldn't think of one other thing it could be. Johnny has a girlfriend, she thought. The words didn't seem like English. Edna woke up from what felt like a very long dream. The truth was Johnny could never like her when there were girls like that around, and Edna was out of her mind to think he did. So what if he'd kissed her? Maybe he kissed ten girls a day. He probably saw Jenny all the time, and he had a life outside the few minutes a week he came to the cabin. It was such a shame to realize this now. Edna still had the entire party to get through. Someone was speaking to her.

"So...so, you must be Edna," Shep Caulfield said when he came back from the bathroom. "Wonderful party."

"Yes, thank you," Edna mumbled, and she rudely walked away from him. She felt like her internal organs were melting. She needed a moment.

"Hey, Edna."

Her face was bright red, but it was too late to avoid Johnny. Frankly, Edna was annoyed. He shouldn't have kissed her if he had a girlfriend who seemed sixteen and whose chest was fully developed. It was horrible of him to have confused her like that.

"The place looks great."

He sounded impressed. Even horrible, and with a girlfriend, he was nice.

"Thanks."

"Do you know Jenny?"

"No, but we spoke on the phone. I saw you at the store."

It took effort for Edna to be friendly. Jenny didn't seem to think it was important to make the same or any effort and offered a blunt "hi" back. Edna wasn't sure what to make of this girl. At Bishop's and now, Jenny was just not good enough for Johnny. Even if they were having a fight, a person has to be able to muster up some kind of outward civility, Edna thought with smug satisfaction, until she realized she sounded like her mother.

Edna had hosted a lot of parties, so she was experienced enough to do it while focusing on every move Johnny made. According to the seating she'd carefully thought out ahead of time and designated with place cards written by hand, Johnny should have sat next to Edna, but when she brought out the iced tea, he was at the opposite end next to Jenny. Edna assumed Jenny moved their seats, but on second thought, maybe Johnny did it. He'd already told Edna he couldn't kiss her, and he came to her party with a girlfriend. Why didn't she take the hint? Freddy and Raul were also in the wrong seats, and their seats were empty. Everyone had probably just sat down without noticing the place cards.

"This is beautiful!"

Laura had a slightly depressing air about her no matter what she said.

"Thank you."

"Hey, you guys are in the wrong spot," Laura observed. "These have our names on them. How cute!"

"Oh."

Raul and Freddy got up.

"No, please sit. Actually, they're just nothing."

Edna grabbed the cards and shuffled them around the table to match where people were sitting. When that was taking too long, she changed her mind and took them away. It was awkward, miserable. She didn't want to sit next to Johnny anymore or let it be known that she ever did. It was good that Johnny didn't seem to notice. He was talking to his grandmother and Laura, and not to Jenny on the other side of him.

Everyone loved Edna's sandwiches and admired the pinwheels and pyramids she'd arranged them in. There were several choices, and she'd tried to make them as exceptional as possible with what was available at Bishop's: a roast beef sandwich with pear slices and horseradish, chicken with bacon, dill and apple, and a grilled vegetable sandwich with lemon, parsley and balsamic vinegar. Proclaiming a favorite sandwich started the conversation at the table. Edna had never seen Johnny eat before, and she marveled as he bit into his sandwiches and politely passed plates back and forth. The basic behavior made him seem well-mannered in Edna's eyes, which lingered on him for far too long. She couldn't help herself. Nothing about this party had worked out except that he was going to be in front of her for a few hours. She could at least look at him. There was no point in planning anything ever again if things could turn out like this.

Raul clinked his fork against his glass, and the table quieted down.

"I'd like to say a few words about the man we're here to celebrate today, our own Zeke."

Oh, right. Him.

The party was for her grandfather, but if it were up to Edna, he would have been totally neglected. She hadn't as much as glanced at him. Grandma at least made sure he had some sandwiches and wine. Grandpa hadn't responded to the hubbub of all these people around him, and he didn't respond when they all quieted down and looked at him. Edna took the needle off the bluegrass record for Raul's speech. By the time Edna found out that Grandma had a turntable, she wasn't even surprised; she just learned how to use it. Grandma only had five bluegrass records, but it was better than her static-filled radio.

Raul was sincerely choked up. He paused to collect himself, and in that moment, everyone was treated to what it sounded like when Grandpa enjoyed his food. He snorted through his nose as he chomped on his roast beef sandwich. He was oblivious to the other people at the table leaning toward him. His snort had a little whistle in it. It was innocent and probably a sign of happiness, but it was nonetheless very embarrassing. Edna should've known this would happen. Why did she tell Grandma to put him at the head of the table? He would have been just as happy on the porch.

Grandpa finished what were thankfully his last few bites, and he zoned out again. If this had happened at home, Edna would have had to change schools. It was hard to believe, but she had created all of this, inviting Johnny and his girlfriend to a gaggle of gray heads, and then showing off Grandpa's table manners. It wasn't some crazy mistake. She'd fought hard to have this party.

"Looks like Zeke's enjoying the sandwiches as much as everybody else is," Johnny said.

A little laughter followed his comment, and it washed the moment away. It was the second time he saved her from something. Edna wished she could take it personally. As it turned out, Johnny was just a nice person.

"They are good," Raul said. "I'm so happy that Zeke has his wife, and his lovely granddaughter with him for the summer. You know, many vets have no one, myself included, who would make such a nice party in our honor, but if anybody should have it, Zeke's the one. When I first came to this desert, I was doing pretty poorly, as most of you know, just running away. Then I met Zeke at the VA. At the time—this was seventeen years ago—he was a little more...more alert,

125

I guess, but he was still pretty messed up, and I thought, here's one mother's more twisted up in the head than me!"

Freddy and Shep Caulfield burst out laughing with Raul.

"Must be some kind o' pretzel in that head," Raul added. He thought he was hysterical. "One of those 'specially, dark kinds, all burnt and crumbling—"

"Raul, watch out how you talk about my husband," Grandma warned.

Raul stifled himself and nodded, suddenly remembering where he was. Winnie and Bill chuckled along with Freddy and Shep, but only to keep things congenial; it seemed they didn't approve of Raul's description of Zeke either. Edna couldn't even look in the direction of Johnny and Jenny.

The laughter trailed off, but one voice laughed louder. Grandpa was chuckling, too. Was he laughing or just imitating the sounds around him or what? It was impossible to tell, and then it was over. The look on Grandpa's face made him seem aware, but Edna thought she could just be reading into it.

"I'd like to welcome Zeke to his own party." Raul said, "And I'd also just like to say that when Zeke was more…around, you know, he had a way of making everyone at the hall feel better, like, if he was there, it was a good place to be. He didn't even know what I was going through at the time but I gotta tell you—"

"Enough yappin'!" Freddy interrupted, and Laura gasped, "Freddy!"

"—this isn't your AA meeting. I'm gonna start crying."

"You don't understand, you son-of-a—"

"Raul!" Grandma yelled.

"Sorry, Mary."

Somehow this had become an argument between Raul and Freddy.

126

"All I gotta say is that Zeke was a great friend at a critical time for me. He understood everything firsthand, and he saved my life. He's a great Marine and a great American."

The sheriff lifted his glass.

"I'll drink to that."

They all sipped something. Edna thanked God that Raul's speech was over. This was turning out to be one bizarre party. She decided to get Grandma's cakes out earlier than she might have done if she was having a good time. Edna had thought her biggest problem with the party would be that it would fly by, but instead she couldn't wait for it to end. Anything less than sitting next to Johnny so they could talk and fall in love for a few hours was unacceptable and bitterly disappointing.

She knew that Grandpa might make the same noise eating cake as sandwiches, and possibly more so. She considered not giving him any cake in that case, but that would be mean and unethical. "Eating cake with people" was the reason she'd argued for this party in the first place. Grandpa probably loved Grandma's Pineapple Upside-Down Cake, so he was going to have some, and it was not going to be pretty. Things couldn't get much worse socially for Edna, but it wasn't like there was a reason to care what anyone at the party thought anymore. It was starting to get dark, and it would be over soon anyway. She turned on Grandma's Christmas lights and raised the volume of the bluegrass record. It might drown Grandpa out.

The music elevated the anticipation of the evening's attraction, which Edna hadn't so much as tasted yet. She hoped she wouldn't hate Pineapple Upside-Down Cake for the rest of her life because it would remind her of this party. Edna was briefly taken out of her misery by how happy Grandma was: she was actually humming while she transferred the three luscious beauties onto china cake stands that Edna dug out of the garage the day before yesterday. The cakes looked just like the picture from 1964, except they were real and in color.

"They're gorgeous."

"If it wasn't for you, Edna, I never would have done this."

It was merely true, and Grandma was very matter-of-fact about it.

"You go out first, Grandma."

Everyone cheered when they presented the cakes. Bill rubbed his hands together.

"I've really been looking forward to this!"

Winnie informed everyone, "He's going off the sugar wagon for one night!"

These people couldn't have been more excited, or at least they had the courtesy to act like it. It was nice. Everyone was so bored in Brentwood, it was impossible to keep thinking of new things to do that would impress them. Here all you had to do was bake a cake. Edna served, looking forward to the fleeting pleasure of standing near Johnny for a moment. While putting cake on his plate, she noticed Jenny's hard stare and, thrown off, she let the gooey dessert tumble onto Johnny.

"I'm sorry!" Edna gasped.

"It's OK."

Actually, it was a mess. Johnny's lap was covered with sticky, sugary pineapple. Jenny held her hand over her mouth, but Edna could tell she was smiling when she said, "Oh my God!" Laura said, "Oh my goodness." Conversations continued after a glance. Dumped cake was not a big deal around here. Edna helped Johnny pick up the mangled stuff.

"Here, come inside," she told him.

He followed her into the kitchen. She handed him a dish towel and grabbed one herself.

"I guess you got me back for dumping that dirt on you," he said.

"No, I'm a clumsy idiot. I wouldn't get you back."

Edna kneeled down and looked distinctly like she was about to clean the sticky sugar off the front of his jeans, but Johnny grabbed her wrist before she could complete the action.

"That's OK."

He took a dish towel into the bathroom.

"Oh, I…"

If Edna had thought about it, she'd never have reached into a boy's groin area uninvited, or otherwise, at this point in her life. She knocked on the bathroom door.

"Johnny, I'm sorry. I didn't mean to…invade your privacy…exactly like I am now."

"No worries."

Edna melted against the door.

"Where's Johnny?"

Jenny held an unlit cigarette.

"He's in the bathroom."

Edna abandoned the scene with Jenny's entrance but heard her say, "Can we get out of here?" before she made it into the pantry. She got the old newspaper article about Grandma's cake and stayed in there longer than she would have if she hadn't been numbly wishing this party away. The bluegrass got louder. It would be so nice to lie down and listen to bluegrass. It sounded like heaven. Edna was exhausted.

When she came outside Grandpa was back in his chair on the porch. Most of the guests were dancing some kind of a square dance. Bill swung Winnie off her feet. Johnny's grandparents were so different than hers. None of them looked like they knew what they were doing except that they knew how to have a good time. Jenny was off in the darkness, smoking cigarettes with Freddy. Johnny talked to Shep at the table. Edna wondered what they could possibly be talking about. She wished she had any confidence that Johnny would dance with her if she asked him to. It pleased her that he was fiddling with a tissue flower she'd made, but not nearly enough. If she hadn't been so shocked and devastated, she'd consider the party a huge success. Even Grandma was having fun: she stood near the dancing and clapped.

Edna was lingering on the porch when Grandpa put his hands down on the arms of his chair and pushed himself up. She'd seen him look like he was going to get up before, but he'd never actually done it in front of her without Grandma's coaxing. He stepped to the railing. Only Edna, Grandma and then Johnny took note of this. He looked conscious. If he was going to say something, Edna wanted to be close enough to hear it. She'd never stood next to her grandfather and looked up at him before. He was taller than she'd thought. He looked down at her and smiled. Edna couldn't tell if he recognized her before he looked away. He put his hands in his pockets and tapped his foot to the music like anyone's grandpa might.

"Grandpa?"

He didn't say anything, but it was a transformation. It only lasted a short while, maybe half a song. Grandpa turned and held onto Edna briefly as he sat back down. She sat next to him quietly, like they always did, only it was dark and they were watching people dance instead of the empty desert. It was the best few minutes she had at the party.

Edna tried not to look like she was focusing on Johnny when she took some pictures later, and after the dancers were danced out, she passed around Grandma's old newspaper article. It was hard to convince Grandma this was a good idea, but Edna knew it would spark conversation about how beautiful Grandma was, San Diego in the 1960s, and how much they all loved the Pineapple Upside-Down Cake. It inspired second helpings and was a perfect way to end the party.

Edna couldn't watch Johnny and Jenny leave together, so she lost herself in the kitchen in the sea of dirty cake plates and baking mess. When Johnny found her to say good-bye, she didn't even look up. She just mumbled "bye" with her eyes fixed on the bubbles and water as she swished the forks around. Before she knew it, she was standing with Grandma as their last guests, Raul and Freddy, disappeared into the darkness on their buzzing motorcycles.

"That was a wonderful party, Edna."

Grandma sounded like she really thought so. Edna burst into tears. As she cried on the steps of the porch, in Grandma's lap, of all places, she realized it was the first time she and Grandma had ever sat together except to eat, and wondered why Grandma didn't ask her why she was crying. That was weird. Or maybe she knew.

"It was very nice of you to make this party for Grandpa."

Grandpa was still there, a few feet away in his chair. Edna sniffed into one of his old hankies she'd bleached and ironed perfectly.

"You've been doing a lot of good things since you came here. The porch looks much better painted."

She'd only painted the porch to make their ramshackle cabin look presentable.

"I can tell you're a good girl."

Edna didn't have either the heart or the guts to tell Grandma that she wasn't—that she'd only had the party because she wanted a date with Johnny and that, in fact, she'd exploited Grandma for the cake. Then she'd clumsily dropped it on Johnny, or, worse, she'd subconsciously done so because she wanted his attention. There were so many reasons she was horrible. She was a deceptive person, too weak to admit it, and her plan had failed. She'd never tried this hard at anything and not succeeded, and the tears burst out of sheer frustration, along with everything else. Edna really had to get a hold of herself. The last time she was this emotional she had to go for a million tests.

"Thank you, Grandma. The cake was delicious."

She sobbed more. She still had a lot of work to do if she wasn't going to be the same girl she was when she got here.

"You were right that Grandpa needed this," Grandma added.

Edna sniffed. She had no idea.

"Maybe."

"I haven't seen him happy in a long time. And everyone enjoyed themselves. That's something to be proud of. I don't think I could have done it as nicely."

Grandma was thinking of comforting things to say. Edna thought she was much better at it than her mother. Grandma didn't communicate much, but when she did, she was focused. And she was right. Everyone did have a good time, except Edna and probably Johnny, the only two people who mattered. But maybe they weren't the only ones. People who hadn't seen Grandpa in years might remember how he ate, but they'd also remember him laugh. And he got to laugh, if that's what it was, and he stood up on his own and tapped his foot to music. In fact, Grandpa was as animated as Edna could ever remember. Her sobs subsided. She sniffed and sat up.

A family of quail ran along the edge of the orange glow cast by the Christmas lights. They moved side to side like a school of fish, kicking up little clouds of dust. A baby quail lagged behind, investigating something in a creosote bush. One of the adults returned for him, and he scampered along.

21
AFTERMATH

The low morning sun bounced off the white sheets standing in as tablecloths and flapping in the breeze. Grandpa's embroidered hankies had blown away and were stuck in nearby creosote and scrub brushes. Ants had found some sugary pineapple on a cake knife, and they were making a treacherous climb up a table leg and onto the sheet. They could only get on when it rested still, without wind. There was an ant traffic jam going up the leg and no exit strategy once they'd made it to the cake knife, but the whole thing was about to end anyway, Edna thought. Life is fragile.

Grandpa stared out into the desert from his chair and tapped his foot again to the bluegrass records. They sounded eerie over the morning wind. The desert, Edna decided, could be as ominous in the daytime as it could be at night, maybe more so.

A few tender words had not turned Grandma into a Chatty Cathy, and they cleaned up the rest of the party mostly in silence. Edna was beginning to grasp that Grandma simply didn't have much to say, and when she did, she said it. She wasn't one to force a conversation. Edna usually looked forward to her mother's postmortem of a party and evaluation of her stupid friends' behavior, but Edna had never been so crushed at a party before. It was liberating not to have to conjure up chat about it while being perplexed by Johnny and Jenny. She was glad she was still stunned and numb, because when reality sunk in, it was going to be pitiful.

Everything she'd done for the last eleven days had been in anticipation of this one night, of spending time with Johnny and making plans to go out together again, if Edna steered the conversation successfully. It was supposed to have been the beginning of the rest of their summer together, not the sad end of it. She spent a lot of time sitting next to Grandpa on the porch, trying to picture and then not picture Johnny and Jenny together. She wasn't sure how she could face Johnny the next time he came to deliver groceries, and it wasn't nearly as satisfying to think about their kiss anymore if he was cheating on a girlfriend when he did it. Or maybe it wasn't the worst thing in the world. No, Edna was sure it wasn't as good.

She hoped that life was nothing if not unpredictable, and that if things were going to change, they would hurry up about it.

Edna might have known that Johnny was unavailable a long time ago if she'd had WiFi. She could have saved herself the emotional trauma and her grandmother a laundry list of crazy requests. Without the chance to obsess about him on her phone, Edna got to know Johnny as a real person, not the social media version of him. She saw how he smiled and how he acted and how cute it was that his eyebrow went up when he was thinking. Her impression of him wasn't based on stuff he bragged about or posted pictures of, or the things he had. Any girl would fall in love with Johnny because of the way he looked, but there were other reasons why Edna fell in love with him. Even if he hadn't been as good-looking, she would have fallen in love with him eventually.

Her grandparents' cabin and its surrounding property had been groomed as if the President had come and gone. Painting the porch, a main activity of Edna's days, was done, and there wasn't a weed left to be pulled out of the ground. If Edna wanted weeding to do, she'd have to start on the rest of the basin. She couldn't languish on the porch for as long as Grandpa did in a day, so a little while after the party was cleaned up, she took a long bath. The bathroom was roomy with a big, old tub. Tubs were one thing Edna liked better old, and she couldn't even tell the water came from a tank. It was an exaggeration, telling her father they had "no running water" here, but Edna didn't mind exaggerating to make a point. The hot water soothed her back, which ached from overwork for the first time in her life. The bathroom window looked out into the wilderness. Edna opened it. The breeze was warm but it cooled her wet skin. The big tub with a view of distant, rolling hills could be a treatment in a spa. They almost never had a good view in the treatment rooms. Edna's body relaxed, but her mind still raced.

The more she thought about it, the less she liked the fact that Johnny had kissed her when he had a girlfriend. She asked herself if this was something to confront a person about, and she decided it was. Johnny didn't say he couldn't kiss Edna because he had a girlfriend; he said it was because he thought she was too young. This wasn't exactly honest. Honesty was important if they were going to be friends, which they naturally were, though it had never been mentioned. The next time Edna saw him, she'd have to clear this up. Edna was able to trick herself into having a reason to talk to Johnny as much as any other girl might.

By the time late afternoon rolled around, Edna was next to Grandpa on the porch again, gazing into the distance like they always did, and the new reality of a girlfriended Johnny had been fully absorbed.

Edna imagined that Grandpa's mind was still, a crystal-clear lake, while hers was a storm, battered with violent, disturbing forces. She tried to lose herself in the sway of a creosote bush or a lizard sighting. She tried to be a crystal-clear lake like Grandpa, but the sinking pull of hopelessness kept winning. Even a cute bunny couldn't liven her mood as he scampered through the scrub brush. Dinner with Grandma was more depressing than usual, and Edna missed her family and escaping into television terribly. In the days immediately after the party, Edna floated between jealousy and sorrow in a valley of despair.

22
THE PINK LIPSTICK NEGOTIATION

The groceries had to be delivered again eventually. Bishop's General had offered remote delivery service since they'd opened in the 1950s. There were always a few customers who were willing to pay extra to stay away from civilization. Until this visit Edna didn't know she was related to people like that. No one told her anything.

Edna thought she'd be off the roller coaster she'd spent weeks on once she knew Johnny had a girlfriend, but adrenaline raced through her when she saw the red truck coming. It raced even harder when he stepped out of it. She was angry at her body for doing this. He waved hello before getting Grandma's groceries out of the back, as if nothing had happened. As if nothing about the way they should relate to each other had changed.

She was sure her mother would advise her not to question him about Jenny. She would tell her that she shouldn't push things. For example, having the party was pushing things, and look how that turned out. But if Edna was crazy when she thought Johnny liked her, she wanted to know. It might help her understand boys in the future. And there was still the issue of honesty between friends. She waited until they were out in the Bronco and some distance from the cabin.

"Why didn't you tell me that you have a girlfriend?"

She tried not to sound too much like a lawyer for the prosecution.

"Because I don't have one?"

"What about Jenny?"

He slowed down on the empty dirt road. He studied her.

"You were jealous."

It was obvious. Edna never knew she had a problem with blushing before this summer. When she got home she was going to look up a good hypnotist.

"Jenny was my girlfriend for, maybe, a month. Last year. She works at the store. She didn't have a ride to the party."

"Oh."

"My grandparents can't stop talking about it, you know. It was nice."

"Thank you. Thanks for all your help with it."

This was mixed news. Mostly Edna was embarrassed, and she didn't like the idea that Johnny had ever had a girlfriend before, though it was unreasonable to think he hadn't.

"You and Jenny looked like you were in a fight. Displaying anger at someone in public is a sign of intimacy."

At least she had a logical explanation.

"She was mad because I wouldn't let her drive. She had her permit taken away."

Maybe Jenny was pretty, but after a month Johnny didn't even like her. Edna was sure of it because there was no way she didn't like him. Edna didn't like Jenny either, and that was before she knew Jenny smoked and had trouble with the law. It made sense. Edna had spent the last several days with a stomachache, conjuring up horrific scenes. She'd never considered that she was wrong about the whole thing. She'd have enjoyed the party much more if she had. This illustrated her main apprehension with boys and love. Once Jenny got out of the Jeep, Edna couldn't see reality. The reality was that a girl slammed a car door, she wasn't nice, and Johnny didn't talk to her. Edna dropped cake on him and didn't even look up to say good-bye. It was awful.

"Oh."

"I can't be your boyfriend, Edna."

"Who said you should be my boyfriend?"

"No one had to say anything."

"Well, I can see how it might be confusing when you act like my boyfriend. When you take me places and punch people if they say something rude about me. And you do nice things for me. And you kiss me."

It was all true. Johnny had never met a girl who drove him crazy, one he wanted to talk to or spend much time with or do things for. Edna was able to be herself more and more with him, and the more she was, the more confusing he found it.

"I said I shouldn't have kissed you," he reminded her. "We can be friends, OK?"

"If you say so."

She wasn't promising anything. Perhaps Edna couldn't talk Johnny into being her boyfriend the way she might talk her mother into going shopping, but she had the confidence of Cleopatra, giddy with the disappearance of Jenny and the fact that Johnny thought about being her boyfriend even if he thought he couldn't be. He pulled the Bronco into the garage.

"I have to wait a couple minutes before I check the oil," he told her.

He was supposed to do that before he took the car out. He was always doing things wrong around this girl. She liked going out, and he'd forgotten about anything else. He put up the hood and realized he didn't need to check the oil, really; he'd just checked it last week. Edna perched on a stool next to him, her foot rocking back and forth like a softly wagging tail.

"What do you do with your friends around here? Do you ride dirt bikes a lot?"

"Sometimes."

"Do you go to movies?"

"Well, there's a multiplex, but it's far. I haven't been there in, like, forever, and there's an old drive-in in town, but—"

"There's a drive-in? Can we go to it? I've never been to a drive-in!"

"I'm not taking you to a drive-in, Edna."

"Why not? We're friends, aren't we?"

"Sure."

"So we can go to a movie. I always go to the movies with my friends."

"Maybe we should just be...acquaintances."

"No, I have an idea."

"What?"

"How we can be friends. Really. If I kiss you and you don't kiss me back, it proves that we can be. That you're serious. I'm not sure you are, but then I get to go to a drive-in movie."

"And what if I do kiss you back? What would happen to our friendship?"

Edna had no clue where she'd gotten this idea or how she'd had the guts to suggest it, but he'd considered it enough for her to pursue it.

"Well, then we get to kiss again, but only once more and in the name of research. I don't think that's going to happen, though. We just have to prove it, and then we're going to the movie."

Edna hated kissing games, but she'd just invented one that worked for her, one she couldn't lose. Whether he kissed her back or he didn't, she was going to be happy with the outcome. She jumped down and steered him onto the stool.

Johnny was beyond kissing games, but he was powerless against Edna's logic. Or he let himself be. He might love her a little. This was a stupid idea.

She rested her hands on his shoulders. Edna finally had him again. This time she was the predator and he was the one who didn't know what was going on. She could see this when she looked in his eyes; she had power over him. She liked this, and she liked her own desire. She touched her lips to his. It felt beautiful, like something she should do all the time. He stayed still but breathed deeply, as if inhaling was a way of touching her. She pressed against him with the insides of her lips, tasting his skin. She put her arms around his neck and caressed the back of his head. She pressed her body against his. She felt sexy;

this was new. He put his hand on her hip at one point and then took it away. The only thing that could explain his ability to keep from devouring her was a deeper desire to show Edna that he was strong and in control enough to take her someplace she wanted to go.

"That's pretty good," she teased, and she kissed him again.

"That's enough."

"OK, but you didn't kiss me back, so we're going to the drive-in movie, right?"

She fell into his arms and insisted, "Right?"

Defeated, he was still thinking about it.

"Right."

"When?"

"Let's ask Mary if it's OK, and if she says yes, we'll go."

Mary noticed that Edna put on pink lipstick every time Johnny came over, and she thought that was fine, but she didn't think it was fine that Johnny had pink lipstick faintly streaked across his face and on the forearm he'd wiped it off with.

"Grandma, Johnny wants to ask you a question."

Edna was loopy. Johnny could ask a question without the help of an announcement. Not that Mary needed it, but it was more evidence that these two had been kissing. Mary was impressed with Edna; Johnny was as good as any boy she could think of. She put down the button she was sewing onto Zeke's shirt and set her elbows on the picnic table.

"All right."

"Mary, would it be all right if I took Edna to a movie? In Desert Palms? It's the drive-in."

"I've never been to a drive-in before," Edna added, too enthusiastically.

Mary studied Edna, then Johnny, then she looked away, leaving them in the awkward silence that Edna was used to but Johnny had probably not experienced. He'd probably never asked Mary any kind of personal question. Edna was amazed at how much power Grandma held in her pauses, and it occurred to her that Grandma might know that. Edna wasn't as embarrassed by the delay as she might have been; Johnny already knew her grandparents, and, unbelievably, he liked her anyway. She found it hard to stand being so in love with him. He looked back at her as if to ask if Grandma was ever going to answer.

"Let me think about it," Grandma said, and she went back to the button.

Mary wasn't sure what she was going to do, but the smartest thing at the moment was to do nothing. Even if she was going to let them go, it was up to her, as Edna's grandmother, to make him wait. She wouldn't answer today. It was no good if it was too easy for anyone to see her granddaughter.

23
THE DRIVE-IN

The drive-in was built a long time ago. Tall, fluffy trees called tamarisks must have been as old as Grandma's eucalyptus trees, and they encircled the property. People camped out with blankets and pillows in the beds of their pick-up trucks. There were only ten cars. Edna thought the place couldn't possibly be making any money. Johnny bought them popcorn at the concession stand, a bare-bones structure that was like the poorer buildings Edna had seen in Mexico. Chubby girls were dressed in pajamas and fuzzy slippers. They talked about the last movie they saw there, and neither of them could remember the name of it. Edna noticed their sparkling, long fingernails as they dipped each already buttered popcorn kernel into a cheese sauce before putting it in their mouths. This would be such a nutritional offense in Edna's world; some parent might be outraged enough to call the police.

In front of the large screen, poles sticking out of the dirt divided the parking spaces. Johnny explained that they used to have speakers that hung inside the car windows before they had the sound on the radio. Edna's stay in the desert had established the longest time she'd gone in her life without looking at a screen. This one was framed by the windshield from inside the Jeep and suspended in front of the stars. Bloodied zombies attacked the terrified inhabitants of a small town. Johnny and Edna cringed as a zombie ate someone's brain. People in a nearby truck moaned, and some girls in the next car screamed. The lucky, young survivors with their brains intact ran away. There was a cough from the backseat.

"Are they gone?"

Mary hated horror films. On the way to the drive-in that evening, she'd told Edna and Johnny that her favorite film was *From Here to Eternity*, and while she knew it was a cliché, she was certain they didn't make them like that anymore.

Edna was infuriated with Grandma's condition that they could only go to the drive-in if she went along with them, but Grandma firmly established that it was with her or nothing. Grandma made decisions, and then she didn't participate in discussions about them, which was totally unfair. Meanwhile, Johnny acted as if it was going to be fun to have Grandma come along with them, and that she was naturally invited. He was either impossibly nice or a little relieved, but Edna would have preferred if he sounded disappointed.

The Jeep had bucket seats in the front and, Edna felt, too much distance between them. With a more discreet seat, she could have hoped they'd hold hands without Grandma noticing, but she had to settle for being near Johnny for the entire movie without touching him. She could see why he had reservations about taking her here alone. It was cozy. Soon their seats were tilted back; it was a more comfortable way to watch the screen. Edna wasn't getting exactly what she wanted, but she knew there was a good chance Johnny would be kissing her if Grandma wasn't behind them. The silliest zombie movie was fun to watch with him because he seemed to think so too.

Johnny liked Edna's giggling better than the movie, and when she sensed this she giggled more freely and let her eyes meet his. She would not be exaggerating if she claimed to have seen the depths of the universe and the passage of all time in their watery beauty. It was a luxury for them to look at each other for as long as they wanted to. It was as if they were finally where they were supposed to be, until Grandma tilted Edna's seat back up.

These two were not watching any movie; they were pickling in their hormones. Edna was annoyed, but Mary didn't care. The young man took the hint, and he put up his own seat immediately. Shortly after, the zombies were blown up, the town was saved, and it was time to go home.

A canopy of stars moved with them down the highway, and Edna loved driving at night with a boy who had his license and a Jeep, even though Grandma was there. She'd been easy enough for Edna to ignore most of the time, except for the seat-tilting part and the no-touching part. Johnny opened the door for Edna to step out of the passenger side and folded down the seat to help Grandma out.

"Thanks for the movie, Johnny."

"Thanks for coming, Mary."

"Can I come inside in a minute, Grandma?" Edna asked.

"OK, Edna, one minute."

Grandma went in without looking back. Edna turned to Johnny. The pull toward each other was natural, like gravity, and neither of them noticed it. The porch light went on, but it was too dim to matter.

"Thanks for taking us to the movie."

"Sure. Did you like it?"

"I liked seeing it with you," she said.

A little smile came to his face.

"But I thought the zombies could have been more convincing," she added.

"Really?"

"I don't think a zombie can jump-start a car. I mean, they're undead. They have minimal faculties and no coordination."

"I think you might be right about that."

"Did you like it?"

"I liked seeing it with you."

He had more confidence than the last time he kissed her. They knew each other, and they knew they liked each other. It was real and mutual and deep. This time Edna didn't think she had to passively let him stop just because certain things that kept going foggy became clear to him. Namely that Edna was still thirteen and that Mary was waiting inside for her. He stepped back from their embrace, but she stayed close, holding the edge of his jacket. She ached to make him stay, to make him kiss her again, but she knew she couldn't force him to do anything.

"Johnny—"

"Edna, I don't think I can see you anymore."

Watching from the bedroom, Mary was surprised at how advanced their affection was, and she would have ended the good-bye if Johnny hadn't.

He drove away as fast as he could without screeching off and adding to the drama. As he looked at the dirt road in the headlights, he understood that even if he had no intention of pursuing anything, there was nothing innocent about being with Edna anymore. It kept ending up like this.

The glow coming from the bedroom disappeared when Grandma let go of the curtain. Edna didn't care what Grandma saw. She didn't care what anyone saw. She watched until the Jeep's taillights disappeared and there was nothing left but the stars in the big sky. Her heart felt so full, it touched every one of them.

24
REALITY

Sitting in the morning sun was luxurious. Edna drank her coffee on the porch, leaving a pink lipstick stain on her mug. She was used to coffee, almost liking it. She was a different young woman in many ways than she had been at the beginning of the summer. She had a tan, something she'd never had before—not even a fake one, because Jill was convinced that was just as bad for your skin. Johnny was a little tan, especially on his cheekbones, and Edna decided that real sun was natural and looked good. Little did Jill know that by leaving her daughter in Dream Valley, she'd turned her into a tanned coffee drinker who'd been properly kissed more than once.

Edna would have gloated that she got better revenge against her parents than she could've imagined by enjoying herself so much this summer, but being in love with Johnny made her feel above all that. Being in love with Johnny made her want to be a better person. She was still daydreaming about their last kiss, though it had been several days since the drive-in. She was grateful that she had so much time to think about it. Thinking about anything to do with Johnny's mouth, his breath, even his teeth, made Edna feel like she was on the verge of passing out, and she thought about it constantly. If someone had told her two months ago that she'd be doing this, she would have laughed; the inside of another person's mouth was a disgusting place to be avoided. Edna no longer knew herself. She had no idea how people in love functioned or went to work or school or were allowed to drive, for that matter.

This morning Johnny would deliver the groceries. There were only a few weeks left of summer, and she hoped she'd get to see him more than just those few times, and then forever somehow, although her vision of this future was murky. He'd said something about not seeing her anymore, but that was small in her memory next to their explosive second kiss. If he had said that, Edna was certain she'd be able to talk him out of it.

EDNA IN THE DESERT

She felt a serene sense of fate, destiny and what's meant to be when the red truck popped over the horizon at the usual time and kicked up its line of dirt across the basin. She would say it was a nice day and ask him if he had a good drive out. It was pretty much always a nice day in the desert, but with her evolved personality, expressing happiness about a typical day was starting to feel natural. While reflecting on this, Edna noticed that something about the truck was different. It was moving more slowly than it normally did. Just like that, her peaceful glow slipped away. The truck had a different driver. It was Ken Bishop, Edna guessed, Johnny's great-uncle. Her soul sank as he approached.

Ken stopped at the cabin and waved to Edna before he got the groceries. Edna couldn't process what was happening. She expected Johnny to emerge from the back of the truck, like a magic trick or some kind of practical joke. Maybe he and Ken had to go somewhere afterward.

"Hi, Edna. I had a great time at the party," Ken said as he approached the cabin alone with Grandma's packages. Edna tried not to look at him as though he was as disappointing as she found him.

"I'm glad."

She hoped nothing was wrong with Johnny, and she also hoped there was a good explanation for his absence, one she was about to find out.

"Is Johnny all right?"

"Yes, oh, I almost forgot."

He turned back to the truck, but, his arms filled with groceries, he decided to make a second trip.

"I got something for you. Let me set these down."

He went into the cabin. Edna heard Grandma say, "Hi Ken." She didn't sound surprised to see him, but she probably wouldn't even if she was. Ken came out stuffing money in his pocket, which slowed him down while he went over to the truck to get whatever he had for Edna. It was an envelope.

"What's this?"

"Well, I'm not sure. You have a wonderful day, now."

He got into the truck and drove down to the garage. Johnny always walked down. The envelope was sealed, and Edna opened it. Inside was a postcard of an oasis, a hand-drawn depiction of lush, green palms around a little blue pond. On the back, it said:

My dear Edna, You know why. J

Edna didn't know what to do about loving Johnny so much, about thinking that he was such a beautiful person. Would she never see him again? Her eyes burned with tears, and she was blinded by a sudden, fierce hurricane in her head and heart. Ultimately, he was honorable and right. In a few weeks she'd be going home and to eighth grade. What could she really do about being in love? She smeared her makeup and saw the black on her hand. She was a wreck. She couldn't look like this if Ken came back, so she dashed inside. Grandma was putting away the groceries. Edna ran into the pantry and slammed the door shut. She fell into another cry, one just as bad as when she first came to the desert. She'd probably cried more this summer than in the rest of her entire life.

She didn't know if she'd ever see Johnny again unless she got lost in the desert and needed to be rescued. She considered this, but it was too risky, and Johnny would only think it was stupid (it was) and then leave again after he found her, just like the last time. That is, if he found her and she didn't die first.

She was at her lowest point when she stepped onto the porch later. The rest of the world sat before her unchanged. It was just another day. It was just another day to a lizard doing nervous push-ups on a rock, and to the eucalyptus trees swaying in the wind. Grandma separated laundry in the back. Grandpa was silent in his chair. A cactus was silent across from him. It was just another dull day that was never going to end. Even if it did, tomorrow would just be another one. Edna was still too emotional to become one with all this nothingness. She needed a sense of closure, someone to fight with and someone to blame. Grandma was all she had.

"Did you tell Johnny not to deliver the groceries here anymore?"

"No, Edna."

"Well, don't you think it's strange that Ken came today?"

Grandma took a moment.

"No."

"Johnny comes every week. Why is it all of a sudden Ken?"

"Ken usually delivers the groceries. Johnny only does it in the summer, this year and last."

"Well, there's a few more weeks left of summer. Why did he stop now?"

"You tell me, Edna."

If she'd been arguing with her parents, she would've had immunity from the romantic element of the scenario because they'd want to act like it didn't exist.

"Touché, Grandma."

Grandma could have said something to the Bishops about Johnny kissing her. Her parents would have, but Edna suspected Grandma was telling the truth simply because she had no need to lie. She was impervious to Edna's verbal combat, tears and temper tantrums. It wasn't clear if this was because she didn't care that Edna was suffering, or because she knew it wouldn't do any good to indulge these tactics. In any case, it worked, and Edna didn't waste her energy. She wasn't entirely sure if she knew the whole story about Bishop's, but she had a feeling there wasn't anything to do about it. There was only going to be another week until Ken delivered the groceries again, and everything else should be perfectly clear.

If she wasn't going to see Johnny again, Edna didn't know what to do with the rest of her life. She sat next to Grandpa on the porch. Did she really have to do anything with the rest of her life, anyway? Maybe she could just sit here like Grandpa and that could be the extent of it.

She wondered what Grandpa would be doing with his life, if he could do something. Based on her father's personality and the stuff in the garage, Edna guessed that Grandpa could host an outdoor/adventure show on Discovery Channel, but she couldn't really imagine what he'd be like. She was sad about her grandfather's condition for the first time, rather than repulsed or bewildered by it. She'd like to have a nice grandpa to talk to. She tried to imagine what he might say to her that would be comforting, but she didn't know this guy at all.

Dinner was at the same time as usual, but the late summer days were getting shorter and the sky was noticeably darker.

"What do you think Grandpa would think of me?" Edna asked.

Grandma considered it.

"He'd think that you're a smart, courageous girl, and he'd be very proud of you."

Edna snorted her juice through her nose.

"Edna!"

"Seriously—"

She coughed. Grandma handed her a napkin.

"I am serious, Edna. Don't be cynical about your grandfather. Or yourself."

Edna caught her breath. She didn't think she'd inspire Grandpa's pride because she didn't see how she had anything to do with him.

"Is that how you think he would say it?"

"Something like that."

"What happened to Grandpa in the war? No one told me."

"Well..."

Grandma trailed off, and she focused on eating.

"Grandma?"

"Edna, I don't know if I know all of it. I don't think I ever will. I don't think your Grandpa remembers it anymore, either. It's all gone."

"What's gone? Grandma...?"

"Your grandpa was missing for a time."

"What does that mean?"

"When he was a prisoner, in the war."

"In the same war as Raul and Freddy? In Vietnam?"

"Yes."

"For how long? How long was he a prisoner?"

"About a year."

"That's horrible."

"It was. Still is."

It took a moment for Edna to absorb these answers. Grandpa must have been tortured. Edna had seen torture in movies, but she always hated those scenes and shut her eyes and ears. She never knew that her life had been touched by a war. If it wasn't for the war, she might be able to talk with her grandfather. If it wasn't for the war, her grandparents might not even be living here. The gravity of Grandpa's situation finally revealed itself to Edna for what it was. Grandpa wasn't some creepy old man, some mentally sick guy she should be ashamed of and try not to think about. He was a man who got hurt, badly. It wasn't the usual kind of sad news that could be twisted with a positive spin and ultimately thought of as for the best later. This was just bad, and there was no other way of spinning it.

Edna realized that Grandma was probably depressed and had been for years, taking care of Grandpa with no one to talk to and nothing to stimulate her. She was probably so used to it, she didn't realize how weird she was. If she lived with them in L.A., she'd be in therapy and on some kind of medication, but Edna wasn't sure if that would be a good thing. They had plenty of room for her grandparents to live with them in Brentwood, if anyone wanted that. Edna didn't know if her imagination could be worse than what had happened to Grandpa, but she wouldn't force Grandma to talk about the war. She hoped Grandma was right and that Grandpa couldn't remember it. Not remembering it was the only good thing about it.

"He got sick slowly, you understand, and then it got quick. He played with you when you were a baby. He couldn't see your brother the same way by the time he was born."

Grandma's eyes filled with tears that didn't shed. Maybe this was as close as she came to crying. Edna had never tried to before, but she wanted to give Grandma a hug. She came around the table, but Grandma didn't move. Edna hugged her from the side, and Grandma held her arm. It was a kind of a hug.

25
DARKER DAYS

Edna spent her final weeks in the desert doing chores, eating meals with Grandma and watching sunsets with Grandpa. Johnny and the war were always on her mind. She hoped Grandpa had really forgotten what happened when he was a prisoner, and she tried not to think about what it was. She tried not to think about the people who tortured him, if they were still alive and who they were. She had nightmares about people intentionally hurting people and about being tortured herself. A gaunt Vietnamese man with breasts sharpened a knife. He was more freakish because he wasn't trying to be feminine in any other way. He was going to cut her fingers off in a dark room without windows. Edna always woke up before anything happened and then was terrorized by the thought that Grandpa hadn't been so lucky.

She had to get out of the pantry after these dreams, and she sat with the stars on the porch. She used to think her mind was tumultuous and that Grandpa's was a crystal-clear lake, but if he had gone through torture, maybe it was the other way around. Or maybe there was no lake.

Edna decided that she'd rather know the truth about Grandpa because then she might stop making up ghastly things. She'd ask her father about it when she got home. Men were never so much in the forefront for Edna. She was usually only occupied with women; she was always in a fight with her mother and spent all her time in activities with girls. She didn't think about what men did. She'd never shot a BB gun or ridden a dirt bike before. She didn't know what it meant when people told her that her grandfather had gone to war.

Edna had already read all the books her parents left for her; Mrs. Anderson and the pioneer women had successfully traversed the country in spite of their many hardships. Edna got the impression that there were many more like them who didn't make it. Apparently there were many cruel hardships in life. Edna had less than ever to distract her from her haunting thoughts about them.

She wanted to talk to Johnny. She missed him. It wasn't fair that he was living his normal life and she was completely isolated without him. She knew it was wrong, but she called Bishop's. The rotary phone took forever to spin back before she could dial the next number. How did people ever live like this?

"Bishop's."

Jenny answered the phone, so Edna hung up. Even if Johnny had answered, she had nothing to say. She couldn't think of anything, even about Grandpa, that would eclipse the fact that Johnny didn't want to see her anymore, and that he'd gone ahead and made arrangements to that end. Edna would hate for him to have to reiterate this in front of Jenny and anyone else who might be within earshot. She wasn't sure if Johnny had a cell phone or how she could find out without asking, announcing to someone that she was looking for him. In all the times she'd been with him, Johnny had never held a phone. It was part of what was so different about him: he wasn't on an electronic leash, always typing into some device like everyone else she knew.

There weren't many names in the residential section of the phone book, but there were lots of Bishops and one John. As much of a man as Edna thought Johnny was, he was still a high school student, and he probably didn't have a phone bill in his name. Still, Edna called John Bishop first. That evening she proceeded to hang up on the nine Bishop families listed in the Desert Palms phone book. Grandma was in and out of the room. Edna noted that she wouldn't mind getting back to her former amount of privacy at home. She almost never had to be on the phone in front of her parents if she didn't want to be.

There was no reason for these calls other than the childish fantasy that Johnny might pick up a phone and she'd get to hear his voice. He'd say, "Hello?" and then she'd say "Johnny?" and then he'd say "Edna..." and drop whatever he was doing to rush over and kiss her again. Then she could talk to him about Grandpa. He might know more than she did. It was an unlikely scene made up by a desperate mind, and Edna was embarrassed to admit to herself that she was doing anything in the hopes that it might happen, only she didn't know why else she was doing it. It was a new low, but these came along so often lately, they no longer surprised her.

She wished she'd thought quickly enough to write a note back to Johnny when Ken gave her the postcard. Someday she'd send him a postcard. She'd mail it to the store if she couldn't find his address, and she'd put it in an envelope so no one but Johnny could read it, just like he did with hers. It would be some consolation if they communicated that way, with drawings and letters written on paper like pioneer people. It would be personal and more private than any other friendship. Edna liked the idea, but at the moment staying in touch with Johnny was just another figment of her imagination. She moped, and eventually settled into a stupor in the dead, August desert. She slept on the couch in the hot afternoons, and watched the sun drop with Grandpa before dinner. A few days and nights passed this way though it seemed time stood still. Slowly, and without her noticing it, Edna's stupor was broken by a growing curiosity about Grandpa.

Grandpa always just sat there. Did he want to move but couldn't? Was his mind tranquil, like the basin he looked into, or a frantic place paralyzed with fear? Maybe there were so many wires crossed that nothing could be deciphered. When was the last time he was more than twenty feet away from this cabin?

Edna tried, with what she'd seen of the town of Desert Palms, to think if they could take him somewhere. That Inn might be nice, as long as they didn't run into any drunken volleyball players or Johnny. Maybe it wasn't such a good idea. She wasn't sure if they could get Grandpa into the Bronco or if it would be good for him to go somewhere, but Edna thought it was worth a try. Grandpa might enjoy a ride.

26
GRANDPA'S OUTING

Quiet as they were, Edna's grandparents looked like any normal old couple in the front seat of their Bronco. It had taken more effort than Mary thought it would to get Zeke out of the chair. He had a pretty set routine; she made him move at the usual times by telling him that it was time to get up over and over again, and by pulling him. It was not a scientific method. When it seemed to sink in that he wasn't going to be left alone, Grandpa was able to get going, more or less on his own, to one of his usual destinations. Edna started to think they should forget the idea of taking him somewhere when he suddenly got going for no apparent reason. He knew to get into the car. Grandma had parked it in front of the porch. She'd shaved his face and cut his hair in anticipation of the trip. The last time he'd been that done up was for the party about three weeks ago, so this was frequent grooming by his standard.

The small church was just up the road from the depressing intersection where she and Grandma had sat the first time they came to town, the day she told Johnny she needed shampoo in Bishop's. Everyone was already seated when they came into the church. Enthusiastic ladies Grandma's age said, "Mary Miller!" and jumped up to greet her, but they were hushed and told that the service was starting. They whispered affectionate hellos. Grandma nodded and directed Grandpa to an empty row toward the back of the congregation, which was a sea of mostly gray heads turned toward them with interest. Edna felt guilty for thinking this crowd was too friendly, like people would seem after taking social anxiety medication, or at least that's how it was in the commercials.

A wizened pastor in an embroidered robe stepped up to the podium, welcomed everyone and made announcements about a bake sale, a youth group and a senior citizens' trip. Suddenly, Edna felt as if she were among actors in the church scene of a TV show or a play, but these people were really doing this. The colorful, stained-glass windows gave her eyes a delightful rush. The adobe interior of the church was white and smooth. It had a graceful, high ceiling, the highest ceiling she'd seen in some time. It felt like the inside of a real building, and it made Edna realize how much she'd been roughing it. There was plenty to look at, but she was careful not to move her head too much and attract attention while the pastor spoke. She might be forced to introduce herself.

The congregation sang along with an encouraging, elderly choir of eight behind the podium. Encouragement was needed because only the braver members of the group sang, and it was pretty spotty. Grandma's voice was low and slightly out of tune, but it was better than Edna had thought it would be for someone who probably never sang and barely spoke. Grandpa remained seated for the most part, but once in a while he stood up and sat down with everyone else. Edna always wanted his movements to indicate some kind of awakening, but they were just never conscious enough to matter. He didn't communicate. At least it was no problem, or not much of one, to take him out with them. Grandma hadn't said a thing about how to deal with him in public. Edna presumed you had to watch him, the same as you would with a dog or a child. It wasn't nice to think of Grandpa that way, but he could walk. He could go off somewhere.

The choir was seated. It was time for the talk, which would be the most boring part of the service, but Edna was so thoroughly patient by now that a church sermon was no match for her Tibetan monk–like ability to endure it. School was going to be a breeze this fall.

Edna had never been religious and had even stopped believing in Santa Claus at an early age. Her parents didn't try to convince her of anything. They took their children to the minimal amount of church. They liked doing other things on the weekend, like playing tennis or going to brunch or almost anything else they could think of. Edna tried to daydream about her favorite moments with Johnny rather than listen to the pastor, but she'd exhausted the topic so completely that it was no longer satisfying, and it hurt her brain. She even missed missing him now. Soon, snippets of the sermon seeped into her consciousness, and she was following it, intrigued by the pastor's charisma and conviction. He put on as good a show as any TV preacher, and it was a welcome one. Edna desperately needed some entertainment.

"—it's interesting that these philosophies throughout the world have different paths to so many of the same outcomes: to be good, and to find a oneness with our Creator. I follow my path to the Lord through knowing Jesus. What the word here does not say is that it's an easy path. You know, it doesn't rate the path as an easy or a moderate or a strenuous hike. It doesn't tell me how many miles it is or what the elevation will be."

He held up his Bible for dramatic effect.

"It is not that kind of a guide book. It wasn't easy for Jesus, after forty days of starving in the desert. Most people, they'd tell the Devil to go ahead and turn that stone into bread. The Lord wants us to live! And if I want that bread so much, if I'm that hungry, then I probably should have it."

He paused and shook his head.

"That's a good one. I hear that one a lot nowadays: 'If I want it so much, I probably should have it.' It's almost funny, if it wasn't so dangerous. Jesus didn't know how he'd ever eat again, but he knew if he ate bread from the Devil, he couldn't still be the same Savior. Now, you can say, 'Well, I'm going to become one with the Lord,' so you see the Devil's bread, you say, 'Thanks, but no thanks, Devil,' it's a no-brainer. But the Lord has provided us with all kinds of temptations, not unlike the ones Jesus had. It's up to us to consider whether, in doing what we do, we remain on the path to the Lord."

Edna had never thought she had that much in common with Jesus. Up until this summer, her biggest temptations were ice cream and the petty satisfaction that came from one-upmanship with her mother, and tormenting her teachers the same way. Both Edna and Jesus had been lost in the desert, but Jesus was lost for forty days and Edna was only lost for four hours. She wasn't sure that the constant ache to be with Johnny was analogous to being hungry for bread made by the Devil from a stone, but this was the kind of thing the pastor was suggesting everyone consider. Everyone had their own individual challenges.

They sang another song before the service was over, and afterward several women named Mary who hadn't seen Grandma in years told her so. There were three Marys and two Kathleens. Edna got tired of being told that she must be Edna while Grandma fielded questions that took her forever to answer, so she went outside to a bench in the shade. She closed her eyes. It had been a while since she'd heard the bustle of people. The sounds felt good. Someone sat on the bench next to her.

"Hi," he said.

She opened her eyes.

"Hi."

This was most likely a dream. Edna resisted the urge to burst into tears all over Johnny's light blue, button-down shirt, and to tell him that she was heartbroken and did nothing but miss him every minute. It would have been cathartic, but she didn't want to embarrass him or her grandmother. At the same time, not doing so felt like lying. She didn't know which was more important, and the attempt at righteousness only confused her. But she was really with Johnny, as she became increasingly convinced that this was waking life. The air was heavy with the nothing they were saying.

"Do you go to church a lot?" she asked.

He shook his head.

"Just sometimes."

"Do you believe in God?"

"I believe in…in something. In doing what's right, and maybe church helps figure that out. Do you?"

"Yes, but I think God is more of an abstract concept than the stories let on."

"Yeah. I'm almost certain of it."

Grandma and Grandpa came out of the church with the pastor, who gushed over Grandma.

"I heard it was wonderful. Such an unusual cake. Everyone always makes something chocolate, but I think Pineapple Upside-Down will be popular and raise a lot of money."

"I just love pineapple," added one of the Kathleens.

Mary saw the young lovers on the bench out of the corner of her eye. She promised to make a cake for the bake sale and said good-bye to the pastor.

"Hello, Johnny. Time to go, Edna."

Mary walked Zeke to the Bronco. Johnny took Edna's hand and kissed the back of it quickly before he left. Again, they didn't really get to say good-bye. Edna didn't know what it would mean to anyway. Nothing less than an earth-shattering kiss would be a reasonable expression of how she felt.

She wondered if other churchgoers could sense their encounter, and if she'd ever been around other people in similarly dramatic circumstances and not known it. She must have been. Of course she had, it occurred to her—with her grandparents. On the surface they looked calm, but theirs was a dramatic scene happening in slow motion. A married couple losing each other.

Edna found it bizarre to feel so strongly about Johnny and not act on it, and she guessed it was just as tough for Jesus, and that was the point. It was going to be more difficult than she thought, being an adult, if it involved controlling these powerful emotions all the time, and she was not looking forward to it. Nothing made any sense. She had no idea why she wasn't going with Johnny wherever he was going, why she wasn't kissing him whenever she wanted to and staying with him for the rest of her life.

Grandpa was already in the Bronco. He didn't move much, but when he did, he was as fast as a shark, as if he wanted to get the event of moving over with so he could get on with his important business of staring into space. Her grandparents always seemed especially depressing after Edna spent time with Johnny, but this time Grandma suggested, "Let's push our luck with Grandpa and see if we can go out to lunch."

The phrase "go out to lunch" was like a remnant from a distant past, and it sounded like a foreign language coming from Grandma. Every cell in her body ached with lovesickness, and Edna was sure she couldn't eat, but going anywhere sounded better than going back to the cabin. She would only look across the basin and envision the precise moment that Johnny's lips touched her hand over and over again. There would be plenty of time for that.

"I'd love to go to lunch."

It was a short ride to the Railroad Diner, which beckoned travelers off the desert highway with a burger special and its classic, train-car look. It had booths and a counter and was in dire need of renovation. The writing on the specials board was faded, it looked like no one had changed it in a decade. Withering plants placed around to liven things up did the opposite. She recognized some of the gray-haired churchgoers from moments earlier, and she scanned the place for Johnny. Mirrors helped her see that neither Johnny nor any other Bishops she knew were there. It was a relief.

They were seated in a booth by the window, which Grandpa naturally stared out of. It was perfect for him: he could look at cars going by for a change. His forearms rested on the table, and when Grandma sat down next to him, he put his hand on her knee. He did it like it was the most natural thing in the world. Seeing him do anything still surprised Edna.

"We always used to sit next to each other like this when we were in a booth," Grandma explained as she looked at her menu. "When I saw you and Johnny on that bench, it reminded me."

"Grandma, did you think of coming here just so Grandpa would put his hand on your knee?"

"Maybe, but I was also hungry."

Grandma's skin went a shade of pink. Edna learned that blushing must run in families and that, somehow, Grandma and Grandpa still loved each other.

"When is Grandpa's birthday?"

"May fifteenth."

"Oh. He's a Taurus."

"I guess."

"When is your birthday?"

"March nineteenth."

"You're a...do you know what you are?"

"I don't remember."

"I'll look it up."

Edna took out her phone. Zeke's hand left Mary's knee. He was making some kind of gesture. Edna guessed it bothered him when her screen lit up, but it had nothing to do with her phone. Grandpa was getting a bus boy's attention. Was it possible? The world suddenly seemed tilted; Edna didn't know what was happening. The bus boy came over. Grandpa cleared his throat.

"Coffee, please," he requested, and he waved his hand around the table, indicating that all three of them would be having coffee.

He sounded like an urbane man, like George Clooney. Satisfied that he was getting coffee, Zeke sat back. His eyes drifted to the window, and he was gone again. It was really hard to tell if he was out of it or if he was just ignoring them, totally uninterested in making conversation. Edna looked to Grandma for any possible light she might shed on this event, but she was just as stunned as Edna was. The two of them waited in case he did something else. The bus boy returned and put their coffees on the table.

27
EDNA LEAVES THE DESERT

Grandpa didn't speak again that summer, but Edna was glad she'd heard his voice the one time. She liked the person he sounded like he was. Grandpa knew that Edna would drink coffee, which was unusual for a girl her age, but he might have been politely ordering for the whole table. He may have had no idea how old Edna was, or who she was, for that matter. She couldn't understand why Grandpa had spoken to a bus boy in a diner but he didn't speak to her or Grandma. Grandma explained that the problems with his brain were so complex that the hundreds of doctors he saw couldn't understand it, so there was probably no way to know. These unanswerable questions drove Edna crazy and they had probably driven Grandma crazy a long time ago. Mary had learned not to take anything about Zeke's condition personally anymore, and she told Edna not to either. Edna couldn't help but think it was better for Grandpa to be around more activity, and Grandma agreed that while it didn't used to be, maybe it was now.

Edna hadn't expected to see Johnny at church, and unlike the party she'd planned, she didn't conjure the outing for the purpose of seeing him, not even unconsciously. She was sure of it. No one she knew ever went to church except on Christmas or for a wedding, and it wasn't her idea to go there in the first place—it was Grandma's. It was strange: she liked that Johnny went to church, even though she never did. She wished she could learn more little things like that about him. She dwelled on how he'd kissed her hand and how now they'd even talked about God, but she knew she couldn't stay in the desert forever, hoping to get a glimpse of him every once in a while. She thought about begging to live here with her grandparents, but they wouldn't even be in the same school. Johnny was going to be a senior and Edna had one more year of junior high.

She'd transformed her corner of the pantry into a cozy nest, and her collections of rocks and weathered glass sat on the windowsill and the shelf below it. She was going to leave them there. It was hard to believe this was the same place she'd at first so despised. She was almost finished packing when she felt Grandma lingering in the doorway. It wasn't like Grandma to linger; she usually either went in or out.

"Hi Grandma."

Grandma had something in her hand, a stack of papers tied with faded ribbon. She sat on the cot and watched Edna pack. There was a quiet intimacy about packing. Edna's mother always watched her pack whenever she was going anywhere. Mostly Jill was checking on what clothes Edna was bringing, but it was more than that. She was holding onto their final moments together.

"Edna, Zeke and I wrote these letters, starting when I was just a little older than you are, when I went away to summer camp and then when he was in the service. You can borrow them, if you promise to give them back. And not to let your father see them."

Grandma had the faintest smile.

"I won't. I'd love to read them."

"You take your time."

"OK."

Grandma went to get them some iced tea.

Most people who were nice were also friendly, but Grandma was only nice. It was important to know this about her. She was actually nicer than many people who were both nice and friendly, so it was worth getting past the unfriendly part. Grandma had helped Edna all summer through the saga of Johnny. She didn't pry or treat Edna too much like a child, with the exception of chaperoning the drive-in movie like they were living in the 1900s. Edna was dying to see her grandparents' letters, but she didn't want to spend her last moments at the cabin absorbed in reading. She saw a little card addressed to her under the ribbon. She'd just read the one thing.

Dear Edna,

I hope you enjoy these and get to know your grandpa through them.

You're so young that I thought it would be good for you to keep in mind this quote: "It is a mistake to try to look too far ahead. The chain of destiny can only be grasped one link at a time." Winston Churchill.

With love, Grandma Mary

Edna welled up, hopefully for the last time of the summer. Grandma was such a different woman than the one who struck the terrifying silhouette on the porch when Edna was brought here against her will two months ago. Edna sincerely hoped that she was also a different woman, and she knew that in hoping so, she probably was. She was glad Grandma had a phone, even though she wasn't likely to be the most talkative on it. Maybe they could write letters to each other. Winston Churchill was last on Edna's list of things to look up. She had plenty of research to do when she got home and questions for her father, and she planned to ask them before she fully assimilated back into her world. It would be a while before this summer left her.

She brought out another chair and sat with Grandma and Grandpa on the porch, watching the invisible balls of wind roll along the tips of the creosote bushes. Her parents weren't coming for another hour. She wished she'd brought out a third chair a long time ago, but it was nice that they were there together now. In any case, Edna knew she'd be coming back to the desert.

THE END

ACKNOWLEDGEMENTS

My heartfelt thanks go to Jesse Greever and Christopher Dixon of eLectio publishing, and to my generous friends and colleagues: Phyllis Azar, Lisa Gallagher, Jason Rice, Reagan Arthur, Daniel Graf, Stephen Visakay, Isa Loveless, Jacey Davidson, and Jillian Steinhauer for their precious time, encouragement, thoughts, and advice. Big thanks also to Tim Sheard and Jim Kaplan of the National Writers Union. I couldn't have written this book without the love and support of my husband and my family or without spending time in the magical Mojave Desert.

ABOUT THE AUTHOR

MADDY LEDERMAN lives in Brooklyn, New York, and works in the art department for films and TV shows. She likes to travel, hike, drive, go out to eat, and be in the desert. You can see what she is up to at maddylederman.com.

CPSIA information can be obtained
at www.ICGtesting.com
Printed in the USA
BVHW041823090920
588501BV00015B/1048

EDNA
in the
DESERT

MADDY LEDERMAN

eLectio Publishing

Little Elm, TX